The Wood Pigeons

The Wood Pigeons

James Davies

Dostoyevsky Wannabe Originals
An Imprint of Dostoyevsky Wannabe

First Published in 2019

by Dostoyevsky Wannabe Originals

All rights reserved

© James Davies

Dostoyevsky Wannabe Originals is an imprint of

Dostoyevsky Wannabe publishing.

Cover design and Typesetting by Dostoyevsky Wannabe

www.dostoyevskywannabe.com

ISBN-9781086559958

For Alex, Kaj and Hugo with much love.

CHAPTER 1

C was in the living room: the windows just big enough to let through the right light, the pictures set where they needed to be and the chairs hard and comfortable. At 9 o'clock D came into the room, sat down and began to read the book that was on the old table. C offered D a glass of wine. D accepted, jovially. C poured a glass too. A warm and zesty silence. An occasional glance up around the room. Candles flickered. C offered D another glass which D declined. D put down the book, got up, left C alone. Now C sighed and gazed through the window. Outside, the sound of the evening wood pigeons was heard. They both loved the sound of the wood pigeons. C poured out more wine and picked up the paper and pen that had been bought as a present. C would write to S. How to begin? It had been so long. It was too tricky. The pen and paper were put down again. No words written. D entered again and wondered whether C had fallen asleep. No. Would D like more wine? Yes, this time. D put on the new pullover. It was not cold inside. C thought how lovely D looked in the pullover and how lovely the pullover looked too. D had other pullovers that C liked. They both read their books. C's book was a famous novel. D was reading something obscure, with a colourful geometric pattern. The candles burned low. One spluttered and turned itself out. C fell asleep. D drank more wine until the bottle was finished. D put down the book, got up and left C alone. C woke up, yawned like a cat, then fell asleep again. D came in to draw the curtains and blow out the remaining candles. D loved the smell and the look of the smoke. The electric light was still on and D turned that off too. D took away the bottle and glasses. The room and C could be seen by the light of the moon. As C awoke, the night turned into the dawn and the hoo-hooing of the wood pigeons began again.

CHAPTER 2

C, in the living room: the windows just big enough to let through the right light, the pictures set where they needed to be and the chairs hard and comfortable. At 9 o'clock D came into the room, sat down and began to read the book that was on the old table. C offered D a glass of wine. D accepted, jovially. C poured a glass too. A warm and zesty silence. An occasional glance up around the room. Candles flickered. C offered D another glass which D declined. D put down the book, got up, left C alone. Now C sighed and gazed through the window. Outside, the sound of the evening wood pigeons was heard. They both loved the sound of the wood pigeons. C poured out more wine and picked up the paper and pen that had been bought as a present. C would write to S. How to begin? It had been so long. It was too tricky. The pen and paper were put down again. No words written. D entered again and wondered whether C had fallen asleep. No. Would D like more wine? Yes, this time. D put on the new pullover. It was not cold inside. C thought how lovely D looked in the pullover and how lovely the pullover looked too. D had other pullovers that C liked. They both read their books. C's book was a famous novel. D was reading something obscure, with a colourful geometric pattern. The candles burned low. One spluttered and turned itself out. C fell asleep. D drank more wine until the bottle was finished. D put down the book, got up and left C alone. C woke up, yawned like a cat, then fell asleep again. D came in to draw the curtains and blow out the remaining candles. D loved the smell and the look of the smoke. The electric light was still on and D turned that off too. D took away the bottle and glasses. The room and C could be seen by the light of the moon. As C awoke, the night turned into the dawn and the hoo-hooing of the wood pigeons began again.

CHAPTER 3

C, in the living room: the windows just big enough to let through the right light, the pictures set where they needed to be and the chairs hard and comfortable. At 9 o'clock D came into the room, sat down and began to read the book that was on the old table. C offered D a glass of wine. D accepted. C poured a glass too. A warm and zesty silence. An occasional glance up around the room. Candles flickered. C offered D another glass which D declined. D put down the book, got up, left C alone. Now C sighed and gazed through the window. Outside, the sound of the evening wood pigeons was heard. They both loved the sound of the wood pigeons. C poured out more wine and picked up the paper and pen that had been bought as a present. C would write to S. How to begin? It had been so long. It was too tricky. The pen and paper were put down again. No words written. D entered again and wondered whether C had fallen asleep. No. Would D like more wine? Yes, this time. D put on the new pullover. It was not cold inside. C thought how lovely D looked in the pullover and how lovely the pullover looked too. D had other pullovers that C liked. They both read their books. C's book was a famous novel. D was reading something obscure, with a colourful geometric pattern. The candles burned low. One spluttered and turned itself out. C fell asleep. D drank more wine until the bottle was finished. D put down the book, got up and left C alone. C woke up, yawned like a cat, then fell asleep again. D came in to draw the curtains and blow out the remaining candles. D loved the smell and the look of the smoke. The electric light was still on and D turned that off too. D took away the bottle and glasses. The room and C could be seen by the light of the moon. As C awoke, the night turned into the dawn and the hoo-hooing of the wood pigeons began again.

CHAPTER 4

C, in the living room: the windows just big enough to let through the right light, the pictures set where they needed to be and the chairs hard and comfortable. At 9 o'clock D came into the room, sat down and began to read the book that was on the old table. C offered D a glass of wine. D accepted. C poured a glass too. A warm and zesty silence. An occasional glance up around the room. Candles flickered. C offered D another glass which D declined. D put down the book, got up, left C alone. Now C sighed, gazed through the window. Outside, the sound of the evening wood pigeons was heard. They both loved the sound of the wood pigeons. C poured out more wine and picked up the paper and pen that had been bought as a present. C would write to S. How to begin? It had been so long. It was tricky. The pen and paper were put down again. No words written. D entered again and wondered whether C had fallen asleep. No. Would D like more wine? Yes, this time. D put on the new pullover. It was not cold inside. C thought how lovely D looked in the pullover and how lovely the pullover looked too. D had other pullovers that C liked. They both read their books. C's book was a famous novel. D was reading something obscure, with a colourful geometric pattern. The candles burned low. One spluttered and turned itself out. C fell asleep. D drank more wine until the bottle was finished. D put down the book, got up and left C alone. C woke up, yawned like a cat, then fell asleep again. D came in to draw the curtains and blow out the remaining candles. D loved the smell and the look of the smoke. The electric light was still on and D turned that off too. D took away the bottle and glasses. The room and C could be seen by the light of the moon. As C awoke, the night turned into the dawn and the hoo-hooing of the wood pigeons began again.

CHAPTER 5

C, in the living room: the windows just big enough to let through the right light, the pictures set where they needed to be and the chairs hard and comfortable. At 9 o'clock D came into the room, sat down and began to read the book that was on the old table. C offered D a glass of wine. D accepted. C poured a glass too. A warm and zesty silence. An occasional glance up around the room. Candles flickered. C offered D another glass which D declined. D put down the book, got up, left C alone. Now C sighed, gazed through the window. Outside, the sound of the evening wood pigeons was heard. They both loved the sound of the wood pigeons. C poured out more wine and picked up the paper and pen that had been bought as a present. C would write to S. How to begin? It had been so long. It was tricky. The pen and paper were put down again. Words written. D entered again and wondered whether C had fallen asleep. No. Would D like more wine? Yes, this time. D put on the new pullover. It was not cold inside. C thought how lovely D looked in the pullover and how lovely the pullover looked too. D had other pullovers that C liked. They both read their books. C's book was a famous novel. D was reading something obscure, with a colourful geometric pattern. The candles burned low. One spluttered and turned itself out. C fell asleep. D drank more wine until the bottle was finished. D put down the book, got up and left C alone. C woke up, yawned like a cat, then fell asleep again. D came in to draw the curtains and blow out the remaining candles. D loved the smell and the look of the smoke. The electric light was still on and D turned that off too. D took away the bottle and glasses. The room and C could be seen by the light of the moon. As C awoke, the night turned into the dawn and the hoo-hooing of the wood pigeons began again.

CHAPTER 6

C, in the living room: the windows just big enough to let through the right light, the pictures set where they needed to be and the chairs hard and comfortable. At 9 o'clock D came into the room, sat down and began to read the book that was on the old table. C offered D a glass of wine. D accepted. C poured a glass too. A warm and zesty silence. An occasional glance up around the room. Candles flickered. C offered D another glass which D declined. D put down the book, got up, left C alone. Now C sighed, gazed through the window. Outside, the sound of the evening wood pigeons was heard. They both loved the sound of the wood pigeons. C poured out more wine and picked up the paper and pen that had been bought as a present. C would write to S. How to begin? It had been so long. It was tricky. The pen and paper were down again. Words written. D entered again and wondered whether C had fallen asleep. No. Would D like more wine? Yes, this time. D put on the new pullover. It was not cold inside. C thought how lovely D looked in the pullover and how lovely the pullover looked too. D had other pullovers that C liked. They both read their books. C's book was a famous novel. D was reading something obscure, with a colourful geometric pattern. The candles burned low. One spluttered and turned itself out. C fell asleep. D drank more wine until the bottle was finished. D put down the book, got up and left C alone. C woke up, yawned like a cat, then fell asleep again. D came in to draw the curtains and blow out the remaining candles. D loved the smell and the look of the smoke. The electric light was still on and D turned that off too. D took away the bottle and glasses. The room and C could be seen by the light of the moon. As C awoke, the night turned into the dawn and the hoo-hooing of the wood pigeons began again.

CHAPTER 7

C, in the living room: the windows just big enough to let through the right light, the pictures set where they needed to be and the chairs hard and comfortable. At 9 o'clock D came into the room, sat down and began to read the book that was on the old table. C offered D a glass of wine. D accepted. C poured a glass too. A warm and zesty silence. An occasional glance up around the room. Candles flickered. C offered D another glass which D declined. D put down the book, got up, left C alone. Now C sighed, gazed through the window. Outside, the sound of the evening wood pigeons was heard. They both loved the sound of the wood pigeons. C poured out more wine and picked up the paper and pen that had been bought as a present. C would write to S. How to begin? It had been so long. It was tricky. The pen and paper down again. Words written. D entered again and wondered whether C had fallen asleep. No. Would D like more wine? Yes, this time. D put on the new pullover. It was not cold inside. C thought how lovely D looked in the pullover and how lovely the pullover looked too. D had other pullovers that C liked. They both read their books. C's book was a famous novel. D was reading something obscure, with a colourful geometric pattern. The candles burned low. One spluttered and turned itself out. C fell asleep. D drank more wine until the bottle was finished. D put down the book, got up and left C alone. C woke up, yawned like a cat, then fell asleep again. D came in to draw the curtains and blow out the remaining candles. D loved the smell and the look of the smoke. The electric light was still on and D turned that off too. D took away the bottle and glasses. The room and C could be seen by the light of the moon. As C awoke, the night turned into the dawn and the hoo-hooing of the wood pigeons began again.

CHAPTER 8

C, in the living room: the windows just big enough to let through the right light, the pictures set where they needed to be and the chairs hard and comfortable. At 9 o'clock D came into the room, sat down and began to read the book that was on the old table. C offered D a glass of wine. D accepted. C poured a glass too. A warm and zesty silence. An occasional glance up around the room. Candles flickered. C offered D another glass which D declined. D put down the book, got up, left C alone. Now C sighed, gazed through the window. Outside, the sound of the evening wood pigeons was heard. They both loved the sound of the wood pigeons. C poured out more wine and picked up the paper and pen that had been bought as a present. C would write to S. How to begin? It had been so long. It was tricky. The pen and paper down again. Words written. D entered again and wondered whether C had fallen asleep. Would D like more wine? Yes, this time. D put on the new pullover. It was not cold inside. C thought how lovely D looked in the pullover and how lovely the pullover looked too. D had other pullovers that C liked. They both read their books. C's book was a famous novel. D was reading something obscure, with a colourful geometric pattern. The candles burned low. One spluttered and turned itself out. C fell asleep. D drank more wine until the bottle was finished. D put down the book, got up and left C alone. C woke up, yawned like a cat, then fell asleep again. D came in to draw the curtains and blow out the remaining candles. D loved the smell and the look of the smoke. The electric light was still on and D turned that off too. D took away the bottle and glasses. The room and C could be seen by the light of the moon. As C awoke, the night turned into the dawn and the hoo-hooing of the wood pigeons began again.

CHAPTER 9

C, in the living room: the windows just big enough to let through the right light, the pictures set where they needed to be and the chairs hard and comfortable. At 9 o'clock D came into the room, sat down and began to read the book that was on the old table. C offered D a glass of wine. D accepted. C poured a glass too. A warm and zesty silence. An occasional glance up around the room. Candles flickered. C offered D another glass which D declined. D put down the book, got up, left C alone. Now C sighed, gazed through the window. Outside, the sound of the evening wood pigeons was heard. They both loved the sound of the wood pigeons. C poured out more wine and picked up the paper and pen that had been bought as a present. C would write to S. How to begin? It had been so long. It was tricky. The pen and paper down again. Words written. D entered again and wondered whether C had fallen asleep. Would D like more wine? Yes, this time. D put on the pullover. It was not cold inside. C thought how lovely D looked in the pullover and how lovely the pullover looked too. D had other pullovers that C liked. They both read their books. C's book was a famous novel. D was reading something obscure, with a colourful geometric pattern. The candles burned low. One spluttered and turned itself out. C fell asleep. D drank more wine until the bottle was finished. D put down the book, got up and left C alone. C woke up, yawned like a cat, then fell asleep again. D came in to draw the curtains and blow out the remaining candles. D loved the smell and the look of the smoke. The electric light was still on and D turned that off too. D took away the bottle and glasses. The room and C could be seen by the light of the moon. As C awoke, the night turned into the dawn and the hoo-hooing of the wood pigeons began again.

CHAPTER 10

C, in the living room: the windows just big enough to let through the right light, the pictures set where they needed to be and the chairs hard and comfortable. At 9 o'clock D came into the room, sat down and began to read the book that was on the old table. C offered D a glass of wine. D accepted. C poured a glass too. A warm and zesty silence. An occasional glance up around the room. Candles flickered. C offered D another glass which D declined. D put down the book, got up, left C alone. Now C sighed, gazed through the window. Outside, the sound of the evening wood pigeons was heard. They both loved the sound of the wood pigeons. C poured out more wine and picked up the paper and pen that had been bought as a present. C would write to S. How to begin? It had been so long. It was tricky. The pen and paper down again. Words written. D entered again and C had fallen asleep. Would D like more wine? Yes, this time. D put on the pullover. It was not cold inside. C thought how lovely D looked in the pullover and how lovely the pullover looked too. D had other pullovers that C liked. They both read their books. C's book was a famous novel. D was reading something obscure, with a colourful geometric pattern. The candles burned low. One spluttered and turned itself out. C fell asleep. D drank more wine until the bottle was finished. D put down the book, got up and left C alone. C woke up, yawned like a cat, then fell asleep again. D came in to draw the curtains and blow out the remaining candles. D loved the smell and the look of the smoke. The electric light was still on and D turned that off too. D took away the bottle and glasses. The room and C could be seen by the light of the moon. As C awoke, the night turned into the dawn and the hoo-hooing of the wood pigeons began again.

CHAPTER 11

C, in the living room: the windows just big enough to let through the right light, the pictures set where they needed to be and the chairs hard and comfortable. At 9 o'clock D came into the room, sat down and began to read the book that was on the old table. C offered D a glass of wine. D accepted. C poured a glass too. A warm and zesty silence. An occasional glance up around the room. Candles flickered. C offered D another glass which D declined. D put down the book, got up, left C alone. Now C sighed, gazed through the window. Outside, the sound of the evening wood pigeons was heard. They both loved the sound of the wood pigeons. C poured out more wine and picked up the paper and pen that had been bought as a present. C would write to S. How to begin? It had been so long. It was tricky. The pen and paper down again. Words written. D entered again and C had fallen asleep. Would D like more wine? Yes, this time. D put on the pullover. It was not cold inside. C thought how lovely D looked and how lovely the pullover looked too. D had other pullovers that C liked. They both read their books. C's book was a famous novel. D was reading something obscure, with a colourful geometric pattern. The candles burned low. One spluttered and turned itself out. C fell asleep. D drank more wine until the bottle was finished. D put down the book, got up and left C alone. C woke up, yawned like a cat, then fell asleep again. D came in to draw the curtains and blow out the remaining candles. D loved the smell and the look of the smoke. The electric light was still on and D turned that off too. D took away the bottle and glasses. The room and C could be seen by the light of the moon. As C awoke, the night turned into the dawn and the hoo-hooing of the wood pigeons began again.

CHAPTER 12

C, in the living room: the windows just big enough to let through the right light, the pictures set where they needed to be and the chairs hard and comfortable. At 9 o'clock D came into the room, sat down and began to read the book that was on the old table. C offered D a glass of wine. D accepted. C poured a glass too. A warm and zesty silence. An occasional glance up around the room. Candles flickered. C offered D another glass which D declined. D put down the book, got up, left C alone. Now C sighed, gazed through the window. Outside, the sound of the evening wood pigeons was heard. They both loved the sound of the wood pigeons. C poured out more wine and picked up the paper and pen that had been bought as a present. C would write to S. How to begin? It had been so long. It was tricky. The pen and paper down again. Words written. D entered again and C had fallen asleep. Would D like more wine? Yes, this time. D put on the pullover. It was not cold inside. C thought how lovely D looked and how lovely the pullover looked too. D had other pullovers that C liked. They both read their books. C's book was a famous novel. D was reading something obscure, with a colourful geometric pattern. The candles burned low. One spluttered and turned itself out. C fell asleep. D drank more wine until the bottle was finished. D put down the book, got up and left C alone. C woke up, yawned like a cat, then fell asleep again. D came in to draw the curtains and blow out the remaining candles. D loved the smell and the look of the smoke. The electric light was still on and D turned that off too. D took away the bottle and glasses. The room and C could be seen by the light of the moon. As C awoke, the night turned into the dawn and the hoo-hooing of the pigeons began again.

CHAPTER 13

C, in the living room: the windows just big enough to let through the right light, the pictures set where they needed to be and the chairs hard and comfortable. At 9 o'clock D came into the room, sat down and began to read the book that was on the old table. C offered D a glass of wine. D accepted. C poured a glass too. A warm and zesty silence. An occasional glance up around the room. Candles flickered. C offered D another glass which D declined. D put down the book, got up, left C alone. Now C sighed, gazed through the window. Outside, the sound of the evening wood was heard. They both loved the sound of the wood pigeons. C poured out more wine and picked up the paper and pen that had been bought as a present. C would write to S. How to begin? It had been so long. It was tricky. The pen and paper down again. Words written. D entered again and C had fallen asleep. Would D like more wine? Yes, this time. D put on the pullover. It was not cold inside. C thought how lovely D looked and how lovely the pullover looked too. D had other pullovers that C liked. They both read their books. C's book was a famous novel. D was reading something obscure, with a colourful geometric pattern. The candles burned low. One spluttered and turned itself out. C fell asleep. D drank more wine until the bottle was finished. D put down the book, got up and left C alone. C woke up, yawned like a cat, then fell asleep again. D came in to draw the curtains and blow out the remaining candles. D loved the smell and the look of the smoke. The electric light was still on and D turned that off too. D took away the bottle and glasses. The room and C could be seen by the light of the moon. As C awoke, the night turned into the dawn and the hoo-hooing of the pigeons began again.

CHAPTER 14

C, in the living room: the windows just big enough to let through the right light, the pictures set where they needed to be and the chairs hard and comfortable. At 9 o'clock D came into the room, sat down and began to read the book that was on the old table. C offered D a glass of wine. D accepted. C poured a glass too. A warm, zesty silence. An occasional glance up around the room. Candles flickered. C offered D another glass which D declined. D put down the book, got up, left C alone. Now C sighed, gazed through the window. Outside, the sound of the evening wood was heard. They both loved the sound of the wood pigeons. C poured out more wine and picked up the paper and pen that had been bought as a present. C would write to S. How to begin? It had been so long. It was tricky. The pen and paper down again. Words written. D entered again and C had fallen asleep. Would D like more wine? Yes, this time. D put on the pullover. It was not cold inside. C thought how lovely D looked and how lovely the pullover looked too. D had other pullovers that C liked. They both read their books. C's book was a famous novel. D was reading something obscure, with a colourful geometric pattern. The candles burned low. One spluttered and turned itself out. C fell asleep. D drank more wine until the bottle was finished. D put down the book, got up and left C alone. C woke up, yawned like a cat, then fell asleep again. D came in to draw the curtains and blow out the remaining candles. D loved the smell and the look of the smoke. The electric light was still on and D turned that off too. D took away the bottle and glasses. The room and C could be seen by the light of the moon. As C awoke, the night turned into the dawn and the hoo-hooing of the pigeons began again.

CHAPTER 15

C, in the living room: the windows just big enough to let through the right light, the pictures set where they needed to be and the chairs hard and comfortable. At 9 o'clock D came into the room, sat down and began to read the book that was on the old table. C offered D a glass of wine. D accepted. C poured a glass too. A warm silence. An occasional glance up around the room. Candles flickered. C offered D another glass which D declined. D put down the book, got up, left C alone. Now C sighed, gazed through the window. Outside, the sound of the evening wood was heard. They both loved the sound of the wood pigeons. C poured out more wine and picked up the paper and pen that had been bought as a present. C would write to S. How to begin? It had been so long. It was tricky. The pen and paper down again. Words written. D entered again and C had fallen asleep. Would D like more wine? Yes, this time. D put on the pullover. It was not cold inside. C thought how lovely D looked and how lovely the pullover looked too. D had other pullovers that C liked. They both read their books. C's book was a famous novel. D was reading something obscure, with a colourful geometric pattern. The candles burned low. One spluttered and turned itself out. C fell asleep. D drank more wine until the bottle was finished. D put down the book, got up and left C alone. C woke up, yawned like a cat, then fell asleep again. D came in to draw the curtains and blow out the remaining candles. D loved the smell and the look of the smoke. The electric light was still on and D turned that off too. D took away the bottle and glasses. The room and C could be seen by the light of the moon. As C awoke, the night turned into the dawn and the hoo-hooing of the pigeons began again.

CHAPTER 16

C, in the living room: the windows just big enough to let through the right light, the pictures set where they needed to be and the chairs hard and comfortable. At 9 o'clock D came into the room, sat down and began to read the book that was on the old table. C offered D a glass of wine. D accepted. C poured a glass too. A silence. An occasional glance up around the room. Candles flickered. C offered D another glass which D declined. D put down the book, got up, left C alone. Now C sighed, gazed through the window. Outside, the sound of the evening wood was heard. They both loved the sound of the wood pigeons. C poured out more wine and picked up the paper and pen that had been bought as a present. C would write to S. How to begin? It had been so long. It was tricky. The pen and paper down again. Words written. D entered again and C had fallen asleep. Would D like more wine? Yes, this time. D put on the pullover. It was not cold inside. C thought how lovely D looked and how lovely the pullover looked too. D had other pullovers that C liked. They both read their books. C's book was a famous novel. D was reading something obscure, with a colourful geometric pattern. The candles burned low. One spluttered and turned itself out. C fell asleep. D drank more wine until the bottle was finished. D put down the book, got up and left C alone. C woke up, yawned like a cat, then fell asleep again. D came in to draw the curtains and blow out the remaining candles. D loved the smell and the look of the smoke. The electric light was still on and D turned that off too. D took away the bottle and glasses. The room and C could be seen by the light of the moon. As C awoke, the night turned into the dawn and the hoo-hooing of the pigeons began again.

CHAPTER 17

C, in the living room: the windows just big enough to let through the right light, the pictures set where they needed to be and the chairs hard and comfortable. At 9 o'clock D came into the room, sat down and began to read the book that was on the old table. C offered D a glass of wine. D accepted. C poured a glass too. Silence. An occasional glance up around the room. Candles flickered. C offered D another glass which D declined. D put down the book, got up, left C alone. Now C sighed, gazed through the window. Outside, the sound of the evening wood was heard. They both loved the sound of the wood pigeons. C poured out more wine and picked up the paper and pen that had been bought as a present. C would write to S. How to begin? It had been so long. It was tricky. The pen and paper down again. Words written. D entered again and C had fallen asleep. Would D like more wine? Yes, this time. D put on the pullover. It was not cold inside. C thought how lovely D looked and how lovely the pullover looked too. D had other pullovers that C liked. They both read their books. C's book was a famous novel. D was reading something obscure, with a colourful geometric pattern. The candles burned low. One spluttered and turned itself out. C fell asleep. D drank more wine until the bottle was finished. D put down the book, got up and left C alone. C woke up, yawned like a cat, then fell asleep again. D came in to draw the curtains and blow out the remaining candles. D loved the smell and the look of the smoke. The electric light was still on and D turned that off too. D took away the bottle and glasses. The room and C could be seen by the light of the moon. As C awoke, the night turned into the dawn and the hoo-hooing of the pigeons began again.

CHAPTER 18

C, in the living room: the windows just big enough to let through the right light, the pictures set where they needed to be and the chairs hard and comfortable. At 9 o'clock D came into the room, sat down and began to read the book that was on the old table. C offered D a glass of wine. D accepted. C poured a glass too. Silence. An occasional glance up around the room. Candles flickered. C offered D another glass which D declined. D put down the book, got up, left C alone. Now C sighed, gazed through the window. Outside, the sound of the evening wood was heard. They both loved the sound of the wood pigeons. C poured out more wine and picked up the paper and pen that had been bought as a present. C would write to S. How to begin? It had been so long. It was tricky. The pen and paper down again. Words written. D entered again and C had fallen asleep. Would D like more wine? Yes, this time. D put on the pullover. It was not cold inside. C thought how lovely D looked and how lovely the pullover looked too. Pullovers. They both read their books. C's book was a famous novel. D was reading something obscure, with a colourful geometric pattern. The candles burned low. One spluttered and turned itself out. C fell asleep. D drank more wine until the bottle was finished. D put down the book, got up and left C alone. C woke up, yawned like a cat, then fell asleep again. D came in to draw the curtains and blow out the remaining candles. D loved the smell and the look of the smoke. The electric light was still on and D turned that off too. D took away the bottle and glasses. The room and C could be seen by the light of the moon. As C awoke, the night turned intothe dawn and the hoo-hooing of the pigeons began again.

CHAPTER 19

In the living room: the windows just big enough to let through the right light, the pictures set where they needed to be and the chairs hard and comfortable. At 9 o'clock D came into the room, sat down and began to read the book that was on the old table. C offered D a glass of wine. D accepted. C poured a glass too. Silence. An occasional glance up around the room. Candles flickered. C offered D another glass which D declined. D put down the book, got up, left C alone. Now C sighed, gazed through the window. Outside, the sound of the evening wood was heard. They both loved the sound of the wood pigeons. C poured out more wine and picked up the paper and pen that had been bought as a present. C would write to S. How to begin? It had been so long. It was tricky. The pen and paper down again. Words written. D entered again and C had fallen asleep. Would D like more wine? Yes, this time. D put on the pullover. It was not cold inside. C thought how lovely D looked and how lovely the pullover looked too. Pullovers. They both read their books. C's book was a famous novel. D was reading something obscure, with a colourful geometric pattern. The candles burned low. One spluttered and turned itself out. C fell asleep. D drank more wine until the bottle was finished. D put down the book, got up and left C alone. C woke up, yawned like a cat, then fell asleep again. D came in to draw the curtains and blow out the remaining candles. D loved the smell and the look of the smoke. The electric light was still on and D turned that off too. D took away the bottle and glasses. The room and C could be seen by the light of the moon. As C awoke, the night turned into the dawn and the hoo-hooing of the pigeons began again.

CHAPTER 20

In the living room: the windows just big enough to let through the right light, the pictures set where they needed to be and the chairs hard and comfortable. At 9 o'clock D came into the room, sat down and began to read the book that was on the old table. C offered D a glass of wine. D accepted. C poured a glass too. Silence. An occasional glance up around the room. Candles flickered. C offered D another glass which D declined. D put down the book, got up, left C alone. Now C sighed, gazed through the window. Outside, the sound of the evening wood was heard. They both loved the sound of the wood pigeons. C poured out more wine and picked up the paper and pen that had been bought as a present. C would write to S. How to begin? It had been so long. It was tricky. The pen and paper down again. Words written. D entered again and C had fallen asleep. Would D like more wine? Yes, this time. D put on the pullover. It was not cold inside. C thought how lovely D looked and how the pullover looked too. Pullovers. They both read their books. C's book was a famous novel. D was reading something obscure, with a colourful geometric pattern. The candles burned low. One spluttered and turned itself out. C fell asleep. D drank more wine until the bottle was finished. D put down the book, got up and left C alone. C woke up, yawned like a cat, then fell asleep again. D came in to draw the curtains and blow out the remaining candles. D loved the smell and the look of the smoke. The electric light was still on and D turned that off too. D took away the bottle and glasses. The room and C could be seen by the light of the moon. As C awoke, the night turned into the dawn and the hoo-hooing of the pigeons began again.

CHAPTER 21

In the living room: the windows just big enough to let through the right light, the pictures set where they needed to be and the chairs hard and comfortable. At 9 o'clock D came into the room, sat down and began to read the book that was on the old table. C offered D a glass of wine. D accepted. C poured a glass too. Silence. An occasional glance up around the room. Candles flickered. C offered D another glass which D declined. D put down the book, got up, left C alone. Now C sighed, gazed through the window. Outside, the sound of the evening wood was heard. They both loved the sound of the wood pigeons. C poured out more wine and picked up the paper and pen that had been bought as a present. C would write to S. How to begin? It had been so long. It was tricky. The pen and paper down again. Words written. D entered again and C had fallen asleep. Would D like more wine? Yes, this time. D put on the pullover. It was not cold inside. C thought how lovely D looked and how the pullover looked too. Pullovers. They both read their books. C's book was a novel. D was reading something obscure, with a colourful geometric pattern. The candles burned low. One spluttered and turned itself out. C fell asleep. D drank more wine until the bottle was finished. D put down the book, got up and left C alone. C woke up, yawned like a cat, then fell asleep again. D came in to draw the curtains and blow out the remaining candles. D loved the smell and the look of the smoke. The electric light was still on and D turned that off too. D took away the bottle and glasses. The room and C could be seen by the light of the moon. As C awoke, the night turned into the dawn and the hoo-hooing of the pigeons began again.

CHAPTER 22

In the living room: the windows just big enough to let through the right light, the pictures set where they needed to be and the chairs hard and comfortable. At 9 o'clock D came into the room, sat down and began to read the book that was on the old table. C offered D a glass of wine. D accepted. C poured a glass too. Silence. An occasional glance up around the room. Candles flickered. C offered D another glass which D declined. D put down the book, got up, left C alone. Now C sighed through the window. Outside, the sound of the evening wood was heard. They both loved the sound of the wood pigeons. C poured out more wine and picked up the paper and pen that had been bought as a present. C would write to S. How to begin? It had been so long. It was tricky. The pen and paper down again. Words written. D entered again and C had fallen asleep. Would D like more wine? Yes, this time. D put on the pullover. It was not cold inside. C thought how lovely D looked and how the pullover looked too. Pullovers. They both read their books. C's book was a novel. D was reading something obscure, with a colourful geometric pattern. The candles burned low. One spluttered and turned itself out. C fell asleep. D drank more wine until the bottle was finished. D put down the book, got up and left C alone. C woke up, yawned like a cat, then fell asleep again. D came in to draw the curtains and blow out the remaining candles. D loved the smell and the look of the smoke. The electric light was still on and D turned that off too. D took away the bottle and glasses. The room and C could be seen by the light of the moon. As C awoke, the night turned into the dawn and the hoo-hooing of the pigeons began again.

CHAPTER 23

In the living room: the windows just big enough to let through the right light, the pictures set where they needed to be and the chairs hard and comfortable. At 9 o'clock D came into the room, sat down and began to read the book that was on the old table. C offered D a glass of wine. D accepted. C poured a glass too. Silence. An occasional glance up around the room. Candles flickered. C offered D another glass which D declined. D put down the book, got up, left C alone. Now C sighed through the window. Outside, the sound of the evening wood was heard. They both loved the sound of the wood pigeons. C poured out more wine and picked up the paper and pen that had been bought as a present. C would write to S. How to begin? It had been so long. It was tricky. The pen and paper down again. Words written. D entered again and C had fallen asleep. Would D like more wine? Yes, this time. D put on the pullover. It was not cold inside. C thought how lovely D looked and how the pullover looked too. Pullovers. They both read their books. C's book was a novel. D was reading something obscure, with a colourful geometric pattern. The candles burned low. One spluttered and turned itself out. C fell asleep. D drank more wine until the bottle was finished. D put down the book, got up and left C alone. C woke up, yawned like a cat, then fell asleep again. D came in to draw the curtains and blow out the remaining candles. D loved the smell and the look of the smoke. The electric light was still on and D turned that off too. D took away the bottle and glasses. The room and C could be seen by the light of the moon. As C awoke, the night turned and the hoo-hooing of the pigeons began again.

CHAPTER 24

In the living room: the windows just big enough to let through the right light, the pictures set where they needed to be and the chairs hard and comfortable. At 9 o'clock D came into the room, sat down and began to read the book that was on the old table. C offered D a glass of wine. D accepted. C poured a glass too. Silence. An occasional glance up around the room. Candles flickered. C offered D another glass which D declined. D put down the book, got up, left C alone. Now C sighed through the window. Outside, the sound of the evening wood was heard. They both loved the sound of the wood pigeons. C poured out more wine and picked up the paper and pen that had been bought as a present. C would write to S. How to begin? It had been so long. It was tricky. The pen and paper down again. Words written. D entered again and C had fallen asleep. Would D like more wine? Yes, this time. D put on the pullover. It was not cold inside. C thought how lovely D looked and how the pullover looked too. Pullovers. They both read their books. C's book was a novel. D was reading something obscure, with a colourful geometric pattern. The candles burned low. One spluttered and turned itself out. C fell asleep. D drank more wine until the bottle was finished. D put down the book, got up and left C alone. C woke up, yawned like a cat, then fell asleep again. D came in to draw the curtains and blow out the remaining candles. D loved the smell and the look of the smoke. The electric light was still on and D turned that off too. D took away the bottle and glasses. The room and C could be seen by the light of the moon. As C awoke, the night turned and the hoo-hooing began again.

CHAPTER 25

In the living room: the windows just big enough to let through the right light, the pictures set where they needed to be and the chairs hard and comfortable. At 9 o'clock D came into the room, sat down and began to read the book that was on the old table. C offered D a glass of wine. D accepted. C poured a glass too. Silence. An occasional glance up around the room. Candles flickered. C offered D another glass which D declined. D put down the book, got up, left C alone. Now C sighed through the window. Outside, the sound of the evening wood was heard. They both loved the sound of the wood pigeons. C poured out more wine and picked up the paper and pen that had been bought as a present. C would write to S. How to begin? It had been so long. It was tricky. The pen and paper down again. Words written. D entered again and C had fallen asleep. Would D like more wine? Yes, this time. D put on the pullover. It was not cold inside. C thought how lovely D looked and how the pullover looked too. Pullovers. They both read their books. C's book was a novel. D was reading something obscure, with a geometric pattern. The candles burned low. One spluttered and turned itself out. C fell asleep. D drank more wine until the bottle was finished. D put down the book, got up and left C alone. C woke up, yawned like a cat, then fell asleep again. D came in to draw the curtains and blow out the remaining candles. D loved the smell and the look of the smoke. The electric light was still on and D turned that off too. D took away the bottle and glasses. The room and C could be seen by the light of the moon. As C awoke, the night turned and the hoo-hooing began again.

CHAPTER 26

In the living room: the windows just big enough to let through the right light, the pictures set where they needed to be and the chairs hard and comfortable. At 9 o'clock D came into the room, sat down and began to read the book that was on the old table. C offered D a glass of wine. D accepted. C poured a glass too. Silence. An occasional glance up around the room. Candles flickered. C offered D another glass which D declined. D put down the book, got up, left C alone. Now C sighed through the window. Outside, the sound of the evening wood was heard. They both loved the sound of the wood. C poured out more wine and picked up the paper and pen that had been bought as a present. C would write to S. How to begin? It had been so long. It was tricky. The pen and paper down again. Words written. D entered again and C had fallen asleep. Would D like more wine? Yes, this time. D put on the pullover. It was not cold inside. C thought how lovely D looked and how the pullover looked too. Pullovers. They both read their books. C's book was a novel. D was reading something obscure, with a geometric pattern. The candles burned low. One spluttered and turned itself out. C fell asleep. D drank more wine until the bottle was finished. D put down the book, got up and left C alone. C woke up, yawned like a cat, then fell asleep again. D came in to draw the curtains and blow out the remaining candles. D loved the smell and the look of the smoke. The electric light was still on and D turned that off too. D took away the bottle and glasses. The room and C could be seen by the light of the moon. As C awoke, the night turned and the hoo-hooing began again.

CHAPTER 27

In the living room: the windows just big enough to let through the right light, the pictures set where they needed to be and the chairs hard and comfortable. At 9 o'clock D came into the room, sat down and began to read the book that was on the old table. C offered D a glass of wine. D accepted. C poured a glass too. Silence. An occasional glance up around the room. Candles flickered. C offered D another glass which D declined. D put down the book, got up, left C alone. Now C sighed through the window. Outside, the sound of the evening wood was heard. They both loved the sound of the wood. C poured out more wine and picked up the paper and pen that had been bought as a present. C would write to S. How to begin? It had been so long. It was tricky. The pen and paper down again. Words written. D entered again and C had fallen asleep. Would D like more wine? Yes, this time. D put on the pullover. It was not cold inside. C thought how lovely D looked and how the pullover looked too. Pullovers. They both read their books. C's book was a novel. D was reading something obscure, with a geometric pattern. The candles burned low. One spluttered and turned itself out. C fell asleep. D drank more wine until the bottle was finished. D put down the book, got up and left C alone. C woke up, like a cat, then fell asleep again. D came in to draw the curtains and blow out the remaining candles. D loved the smell and the look of the smoke. The electric light was still on and D turned that off too. D took away the bottle and glasses. The room and C could be seen by the light of the moon. As C awoke, the night turned and the hoo-hooing began again.

CHAPTER 28

In the living room: the windows just big enough to let through the right light, the pictures set where they needed to be and the chairs hard and comfortable. At 9 o'clock D came into the room, sat down and began to read the book that was on the old table. C offered D a glass of wine. D accepted. C poured a glass too. Silence. An occasional glance up around the room. Candles flickered. C offered D another glass which D declined. D put down the book, got up, left C alone. Now C sighed through the window. Outside, the sound of the evening wood was heard. They both loved the sound of the wood. C poured out more wine and picked up the paper and pen that had been bought as a present. C would write to S. How to begin? It had been so long. It was tricky. The pen and paper down again. Words written. D entered again and C had fallen asleep. Would D like more wine? Yes, this time. D put on the pullover. It was not cold inside. C thought how lovely D looked and how the pullover looked too. Pullovers. They both read their books. C's book was a novel. D was reading something obscure, with a geometric pattern. The candles burned low. One spluttered and turned itself out. C fell asleep. D drank more wine until the bottle was finished. D put down the book, got up and left C alone. C woke up then fell asleep again. D came in to draw the curtains and blow out the remaining candles. D loved the smell and the look of the smoke. The electric light was still on and D turned that off too. D took away the bottle and glasses. The room and C could be seen by the light of the moon. As C awoke, the night turned and the hoo-hooing began again.

CHAPTER 29

In the living room: the windows just big enough to let through the right light, the pictures set where they needed to be and the chairs hard and comfortable. At 9 o'clock D came into the room, sat down and began to read the book that was on the old table. C offered D a glass of wine. D accepted. C poured a glass too. Silence. An occasional glance up around the room. Candles flickered. C offered D another glass which D declined. D put down the book, got up, left C alone. Now C sighed through the window. Outside, the sound of the evening wood was heard. They both loved the sound of the wood. C poured out more wine and picked up the paper and pen that had been bought as a present. C would write to S. How to begin? It had been so long. It was tricky. The pen and paper down again. Words written. D entered again and C had fallen asleep. Would D like more wine? Yes, this time. D put on the pullover. It was not cold inside. C thought how lovely D looked and how the pullover looked too. Pullovers. They both read their books. C's book was a novel. D was reading something obscure, with a geometric pattern. The candles burned low. One spluttered and turned itself out. C fell asleep. D drank more wine until the bottle was finished. D put down the book, got up and left C alone. C woke up then fell asleep again. D came in to draw the curtains and blow out the remaining candles. D loved the smell and the look of the smoke. The electric light was on and D turned that off too. D took away the bottle and glasses. The room and C could be seen by the light of the moon. As C awoke, the night turned and the hoo-hooing began again.

CHAPTER 30

In the living room: the windows just big enough to let through the right light, the pictures set where they needed to be and the chairs hard and comfortable. At 9 o'clock D came into the room, sat down and began to read the book that was on the old table. C offered D a glass of wine. D accepted. C poured a glass too. Silence. An occasional glance up around the room. Candles flickered. C offered D another glass which D declined. D put down the book, got up, left C alone. Now C sighed through the window. Outside, the sound of the evening wood was heard. They both loved the sound of the wood. C poured out more wine and picked up the paper and pen that had been bought as a present. C would write to S. How to begin? It had been so long. It was tricky. The pen and paper down again. Words written. D entered again and C had fallen asleep. Would D like more wine? Yes, this time. D put on the pullover. It was not cold inside. C thought how D looked and how the pullover looked too. Pullovers. They both read their books. C's book was a novel. D was reading something obscure, with a geometric pattern. The candles burned low. One spluttered and turned itself out. C fell asleep. D drank more wine until the bottle was finished. D put down the book, got up and left C alone. C woke up then fell asleep again. D came in to draw the curtains and blow out the remaining candles. D loved the smell and the look of the smoke. The electric light was on and D turned that off too. D took away the bottle and glasses. The room and C could be seen by the light of the moon. As C awoke, the night turned and the hoo-hooing began again.

CHAPTER 31

In the living room: the windows big enough to let through the right light, the pictures set where they needed to be and the chairs hard and comfortable. At 9 o'clock D came into the room, sat down and began to read the book that was on the old table. C offered D a glass of wine. D accepted. C poured a glass too. Silence. An occasional glance up around the room. Candles flickered. C offered D another glass which D declined. D put down the book, got up, left C alone. Now C sighed through the window. Outside, the sound of the evening wood was heard. They both loved the sound of the wood. C poured out more wine and picked up the paper and pen that had been bought as a present. C would write to S. How to begin? It had been so long. It was tricky. The pen and paper down again. Words written. D entered again and C had fallen asleep. Would D like more wine? Yes, this time. D put on the pullover. It was not cold inside. C thought how D looked and how the pullover looked too. Pullovers. They both read their books. C's book was a novel. D was reading something obscure, with a geometric pattern. The candles burned low. One spluttered and turned itself out. C fell asleep. D drank more wine until the bottle was finished. D put down the book, got up and left C alone. C woke up then fell asleep again. D came in to draw the curtains and blow out the remaining candles. D loved the smell and the look of the smoke. The electric light was on and D turned that off too. D took away the bottle and glasses. The room and C could be seen by the light of the moon. As C awoke, the night turned and the hoo-hooing began again.

CHAPTER 32

In the living room: the windows big enough to let through the right light, the pictures set where they needed to be and the chairs hard and comfortable. At 9 o'clock D came into the room, sat down and began to read the book that was on the old table. C offered D a glass of wine. D accepted. C poured a glass too. Silence. An occasional glance up around the room. Candles flickered. C offered D another glass which D declined. D put down the book, got up, left C alone. Now C sighed through the window. Outside, the sound of the evening wood was heard. They both loved the sound of the wood. C poured out more wine and picked up the paper and pen that had been bought as a present. C would write to S. How to begin? It had been so long. It was tricky. The pen and paper down again. Words written. D entered again and C had fallen asleep. Would D like more wine? Yes, this time. D put on the pullover. It was not cold inside. C thought how D looked and how the pullover looked too. They both read their books. C's book was a novel. D was reading something obscure, with a geometric pattern. The candles burned low. One spluttered and turned itself out. C fell asleep. D drank more wine until the bottle was finished. D put down the book, got up and left C alone. C woke up then fell asleep again. D came in to draw the curtains and blow out the remaining candles. D loved the smell and the look of the smoke. The electric light was on and D turned that off too. D took away the bottle and glasses. The room and C could be seen by the light of the moon. As C awoke, the night turned and the hoo-hooing began again.

CHAPTER 33

In the living room: the windows big enough to let through the right light, the pictures set where they needed to be and the chairs hard and comfortable. At 9 o'clock D came into the room, sat down and began to read the book that was on the old table. C offered D a glass of wine. D accepted. C poured a glass too. Silence. An occasional glance up around the room. Candles flickered. C offered D another glass which D declined. D put down the book, got up, left C alone. Now C sighed through the window. Outside, the sound of the evening wood was heard. They both loved the sound of the wood. C poured out more wine and picked up the paper and pen that had been bought as a present. C would write to S. How to begin? It had been so long. It was tricky. The pen and paper down again. Words written. D entered again and C had fallen asleep. Would D like more wine? Yes, this time. D put on the pullover. It was not cold inside. C thought how D looked and how the pullover looked too. They both read their books. C's book was a novel. D was reading something obscure, with a geometric pattern. The candles burned low. One spluttered, turned itself out. C fell asleep. D drank more wine until the bottle was finished. D put down the book, got up and left C alone. C woke up then fell asleep again. D came in to draw the curtains and blow out the remaining candles. D loved the smell and the look of the smoke. The electric light was on and D turned that off too. D took away the bottle and glasses. The room and C could be seen by the light of the moon. As C awoke, the night turned and the hoo-hooing began again.

CHAPTER 34

In the living room: the windows big enough to let through the right light, the pictures set where they needed to be and the chairs hard and comfortable. At 9 o'clock D came into the room, sat down and began to read the book that was on the old table. C offered D a glass of wine. D accepted. C poured a glass too. Silence. An occasional glance up around the room. Candles flickered. C offered D another glass which D declined. D put down the book, got up, left C alone. Now C sighed through the window. Outside, the sound of the evening wood was heard. They both loved the sound of the wood. C poured out more wine and picked up the paper and pen that had been bought as a present. C would write to S. How to begin? It had been so long. It was tricky. The pen and paper down again. Words written. D entered again and C had fallen asleep. Would D like more wine? Yes, this time. D put on the pullover. It was not cold inside. C thought how D looked and how the pullover looked too. They both read their books. C's book was a novel. D was reading something obscure, with a geometric pattern. The candles burned low. One spluttered, turned itself out. C fell asleep. D drank more wine until the bottle was finished. D put down the book and left C alone. C woke up then fell asleep again. D came in to draw the curtains and blow out the remaining candles. D loved the smell and the look of the smoke. The electric light was on and D turned that off too. D took away the bottle and glasses. The room and C could be seen by the light of the moon. As C awoke, the night turned and the hoo-hooing began again.

CHAPTER 35

In the living room: the windows big enough to let through the right light, the pictures set where they needed to be and the chairs hard and comfortable. At 9 o'clock D came into the room, sat down and began to read the book that was on the old table. C offered D a glass of wine. D accepted. C poured a glass too. Silence. An occasional glance up around the room. Candles flickered. C offered D another glass which D declined. D put down the book, got up, left C alone. Now C sighed through the window. Outside, the sound of the evening wood was heard. They both loved the sound of the wood. C poured out more wine and picked up the paper and pen that had been bought as a present. C would write to S. How to begin? It had been so long. It was tricky. The pen and paper down again. D entered again and C had fallen asleep. Would D like more wine? Yes, this time. D put on the pullover. It was not cold inside. C thought how D looked and how the pullover looked too. They both read their books. C's book was a novel. D was reading something obscure, with a geometric pattern. The candles burned low. One spluttered, turned itself out. C fell asleep. D drank more wine until the bottle was finished. D put down the book and left C alone. C woke up then fell asleep again. D came in to draw the curtains and blow out the remaining candles. D loved the smell and the look of the smoke. The electric light was on and D turned that off too. D took away the bottle and glasses. The room and C could be seen by the light of the moon. As C awoke, the night turned and the hoo-hooing began again.

CHAPTER 36

In the living room: the windows big enough to let through the right light, the pictures set where they needed to be and the chairs hard and comfortable. At 9 o'clock D came into the room, sat down and began to read the book that was on the old table. C offered D a glass of wine. D accepted. C poured a glass too. Silence. An occasional glance up around the room. Candles flickered. C offered D another glass which D declined. D put down the book, got up, left C alone. Now C sighed through the window. Outside, the sound of the evening wood was heard. They both loved the sound of the wood. C poured out more wine and picked up the paper and pen that had been bought as a present. C would write to S. How to begin? It had been so long. It was tricky. The pen and paper down again. D entered again and C had fallen asleep. Would D like more wine? Yes, this time. D put on the pullover. It was not cold inside. C thought how D looked and how the pullover looked too. They both read their books. C's book was a novel. D was reading something obscure, with a geometric pattern. The candles burned low. One spluttered, turned itself out. C fell asleep. D drank more wine until the bottle was finished. D put down the book and left C alone. C woke up then fell asleep. D came in to draw the curtains and blow out the remaining candles. D loved the smell and the look of the smoke. The electric light was on and D turned that off too. D took away the bottle and glasses. The room and C could be seen by the light of the moon. As C awoke, the night turned and the hoo-hooing began again.

CHAPTER 37

In the living room: the windows big enough to let through the right light, the pictures set where they needed to be and the chairs hard and comfortable. At 9 o'clock D came into the room, sat down and began to read the book that was on the old table. C offered D a glass of wine. D accepted. C poured a glass too. Silence. An occasional glance up around the room. Candles flickered. C offered D another glass which D declined. D put down the book, got up, left C alone. Now C sighed through the window. Outside, the sound of the evening wood was heard. They both loved the sound of the wood. C poured out more wine and picked up the paper and pen that had been bought as a present. C would write to S. How to begin? It had been so long. It was tricky. The pen and paper down again. D entered again and C had fallen asleep. Would D like more wine? Yes, this time. D put on the pullover. It was not cold inside. C thought how D looked and how the pullover looked too. They both read their books. C's book was a novel. D was reading something obscure, with a geometric pattern. The candles burned low. One spluttered, turned itself out. C fell asleep. D drank more wine until the bottle was finished. D put down the book and left C alone. C woke up then fell. D came in to draw the curtains and blow out the remaining candles. D loved the smell and the look of the smoke. The electric light was on and D turned that off too. D took away the bottle and glasses. The room and C could be seen by the light of the moon. As C awoke, the night turned and the hoo-hooing began again.

CHAPTER 38

In the living room: windows big enough to let through the right light, the pictures set where they needed to be and the chairs hard and comfortable. At 9 o'clock D came into the room, sat down and began to read the book that was on the old table. C offered D a glass of wine. D accepted. C poured a glass too. Silence. An occasional glance up around the room. Candles flickered. C offered D another glass which D declined. D put down the book, got up, left C alone. Now C sighed through the window. Outside, the sound of the evening wood was heard. They both loved the sound of the wood. C poured out more wine and picked up the paper and pen that had been bought as a present. C would write to S. How to begin? It had been so long. It was tricky. The pen and paper down again. D entered again and C had fallen asleep. Would D like more wine? Yes, this time. D put on the pullover. It was not cold inside. C thought how D looked and how the pullover looked too. They both read their books. C's book was a novel. D was reading something obscure, with a geometric pattern. The candles burned low. One spluttered, turned itself out. C fell asleep. D drank more wine until the bottle was finished. D put down the book and left C alone. C woke up then fell. D came in to draw the curtains and blow out the remaining candles. D loved the smell and the look of the smoke. The electric light was on and D turned that off too. D took away the bottle and glasses. The room and C could be seen by the light of the moon. As C awoke, the night turned and the hoo-hooing began again.

CHAPTER 39

In the living room: windows big enough to let through the right light, the pictures set where they needed to be and the chairs hard and comfortable. At 9 o'clock D came into the room, sat down and began to read the book that was on the old table. C offered D a glass of wine. D accepted. C poured a glass. Silence. An occasional glance up around the room. Candles flickered. C offered D another glass which D declined. D put down the book, got up, left C alone. Now C sighed through the window. Outside, the sound of the evening wood was heard. They both loved the sound of the wood. C poured out more wine and picked up the paper and pen that had been bought as a present. C would write to S. How to begin? It had been so long. It was tricky. The pen and paper down again. D entered again and C had fallen asleep. Would D like more wine? Yes, this time. D put on the pullover. It was not cold inside. C thought how D looked and how the pullover looked too. They both read their books. C's book was a novel. D was reading something obscure, with a geometric pattern. The candles burned low. One spluttered, turned itself out. C fell asleep. D drank more wine until the bottle was finished. D put down the book and left C alone. C woke up then fell. D came in to draw the curtains and blow out the remaining candles. D loved the smell and the look of the smoke. The electric light was on and D turned that off too. D took away the bottle and glasses. The room and C could be seen by the light of the moon. As C awoke, the night turned and the hoo-hooing began again.

CHAPTER 40

In the living room: windows big enough to let through the right light, the pictures set where they needed to be and the chairs hard and comfortable. At 9 o'clock D came into the room, sat down and began to read the book that was on the old table. C offered D a glass of wine. D accepted. C poured. Silence. An occasional glance up around the room. Candles flickered. C offered D another glass which D declined. D put down the book, got up, left C alone. Now C sighed through the window. Outside, the sound of the evening wood was heard. They both loved the sound of the wood. C poured out more wine and picked up the paper and pen that had been bought as a present. C would write to S. How to begin? It had been so long. It was tricky. The pen and paper down again. D entered again and C had fallen asleep. Would D like more wine? Yes, this time. D put on the pullover. It was not cold inside. C thought how D looked and how the pullover looked too. They both read their books. C's book was a novel. D was reading something obscure, with a geometric pattern. The candles burned low. One spluttered, turned itself out. C fell asleep. D drank more wine until the bottle was finished. D put down the book and left C alone. C woke up then fell. D came in to draw the curtains and blow out the remaining candles. D loved the smell and the look of the smoke. The electric light was on and D turned that off too. D took away the bottle and glasses. The room and C could be seen by the light of the moon. As C awoke, the night turned and the hoo-hooing began again.

CHAPTER 41

In the living room: windows big enough to let through the right light, the pictures set where they needed to be and the chairs hard and comfortable. At 9 o'clock D came into the room, sat down and began to read the book that was on the old table. C offered D a glass of wine. D accepted. C poured. Silence. An occasional glance up around the room. Candles flickered. C offered D another glass which D declined. D put down the book, got up, left C alone. Now C sighed through the window. Outside, the sound of the evening wood was heard. They both loved the sound of the wood. C poured out more wine and picked up the paper and pen that had been bought as a present. C would write to S. How to begin? It had been so long. It was tricky. The pen and paper down again. D entered again and C had fallen asleep. Would D like more wine? Yes, this time. D put on the pullover. It was not cold inside. C thought how D looked and how the pullover looked too. They both read their books. C's book was a novel. D was reading something obscure, with a geometric pattern. The candles burned low. One spluttered, turned itself out. C fell asleep. D drank wine until the bottle was finished. D put down the book and left C alone. C woke up then fell. D came in to draw the curtains and blow out the remaining candles. D loved the smell and the look of the smoke. The electric light was on and D turned that off too. D took away the bottle and glasses. The room and C could be seen by the light of the moon. As C awoke, the night turned and the hoo-hooing began again.

CHAPTER 42

In the living room: windows big enough to let through the right light, the pictures where they needed to be and the chairs hard and comfortable. At 9 o'clock D came into the room, sat down and began to read the book that was on the old table. C offered D a glass of wine. D accepted. C poured. Silence. An occasional glance up around the room. Candles flickered. C offered D another glass which D declined. D put down the book, got up, left C alone. Now C sighed through the window. Outside, the sound of the evening wood was heard. They both loved the sound of the wood. C poured out more wine and picked up the paper and pen that had been bought as a present. C would write to S. How to begin? It had been so long. It was tricky. The pen and paper down again. D entered again and C had fallen asleep. Would D like more wine? Yes, this time. D put on the pullover. It was not cold inside. C thought how D looked and how the pullover looked too. They both read their books. C's book was a novel. D was reading something obscure, with a geometric pattern. The candles burned low. One spluttered, turned itself out. C fell asleep. D drank wine until the bottle was finished. D put down the book and left C alone. C woke up then fell. D came in to draw the curtains and blow out the remaining candles. D loved the smell and the look of the smoke. The electric light was on and D turned that off too. D took away the bottle and glasses. The room and C could be seen by the light of the moon. As C awoke, the night turned and the hoo-hooing began again.

CHAPTER 43

In the living room: windows big enough to let through the right light, the pictures where they needed to be and the chairs hard and comfortable. At 9 o'clock D came into the room, sat down and began to read the book that was on the old table. C offered D a glass of wine. D accepted. C poured. Silence. An occasional glance up around the room. Candles flickered. C offered D another glass which D declined. D put down the book, got up, left C alone. Now C sighed through the window. Outside, the sound of the evening wood was heard. They both loved the sound of the wood. C poured out more wine and picked up the paper and pen that had been bought as a present. C would write to S. How to begin? It had been so long. It was tricky. The pen and paper down again. D entered again and C had fallen asleep. Would D like more wine? Yes, this time. D put on the pullover. It was not cold inside. C thought how D looked and how the pullover looked too. They both read their books. C's book was a novel. D was reading something obscure, with a geometric pattern. The candles burned low. One spluttered, turned itself out. C fell asleep. D drank wine until the bottle was finished. D put down the book and left C alone. C woke up then fell. D came in to draw the curtains and blow out the remaining candles. D loved the smell and the look of the smoke. The electric light was on and D turned that off too. D took away the bottle and glasses. C could be seen by the light of the moon. As C awoke, the night turned and the hoo-hooing began again.

CHAPTER 44

In the living room: windows big enough to let through the right light, the pictures where they needed to be and the chairs hard and comfortable. At 9 o'clock D came into the room, sat down and began to read the book that was on the old table. C offered D a glass of wine. D accepted. C poured. Silence. An occasional glance up around the room. Candles flickered. C offered D another glass which D declined. D put down the book, got up, left C alone. Now C sighed. Outside, the sound of the evening wood was heard. They both loved the sound of the wood. C poured out more wine and picked up the paper and pen that had been bought as a present. C would write to S. How to begin? It had been so long. It was tricky. The pen and paper down again. D entered again and C had fallen asleep. Would D like more wine? Yes, this time. D put on the pullover. It was not cold inside. C thought how D looked and how the pullover looked too. They both read their books. C's book was a novel. D was reading something obscure, with a geometric pattern. The candles burned low. One spluttered, turned itself out. C fell asleep. D drank wine until the bottle was finished. D put down the book and left C alone. C woke up then fell. D came in to draw the curtains and blow out the remaining candles. D loved the smell and the look of the smoke. The electric light was on and D turned that off too. D took away the bottle and glasses. C could be seen by the light of the moon. As C awoke, the night turned and the hoo-hooing began again.

CHAPTER 45

In the living room: windows big enough to let through the right light, the pictures where they needed to be and the chairs hard and comfortable. At 9 o'clock D came into the room, sat down and began to read the book that was on the old table. C offered D a glass of wine. D accepted. C poured. Silence. An occasional glance up around the room. Candles flickered. C offered D another glass which D declined. D put down the book, got up, left C alone. Now C sighed. Outside, the sound of the evening wood was heard. They both loved the sound of the wood. C poured out more wine and picked up the paper and pen that had been bought as a present. C would write to S. How to begin? It had been so long. It was tricky. The pen and paper down again. D entered again and C had fallen asleep. Would D like more wine? Yes, this time. D put on the pullover. It was not cold inside. C thought how D looked and how the pullover looked too. They both read their books. C's book was a novel. D was reading something obscure, with a geometric pattern. The candles burned. One spluttered, turned itself out. C fell asleep. D drank wine until the bottle was finished. D put down the book and left C alone. C woke up then fell. D came in to draw the curtains and blow out the remaining candles. D loved the smell and the look of the smoke. The electric light was on and D turned that off too. D took away the bottle and glasses. C could be seen by the light of the moon. As C awoke, the night turned and the hoo-hooing began again.

CHAPTER 46

In the living room: windows big enough to let through the right light, the pictures where they needed to be and the chairs hard and comfortable. At 9 o'clock D came into the room, sat down and began to read the book that was on the old table. C offered D a glass of wine. D accepted. C poured. Silence. An occasional glance up around the room. Candles flickered. C offered D another glass which D declined. D put down the book, got up, left C alone. Now C sighed. Outside, the sound of the evening wood was heard. The sound of the wood. C poured out more wine and picked up the paper and pen that had been bought as a present. C would write to S. How to begin? It had been so long. It was tricky. The pen and paper down again. D entered again and C had fallen asleep. Would D like more wine? Yes, this time. D put on the pullover. It was not cold inside. C thought how D looked and how the pullover looked too. They both read their books. C's book was a novel. D was reading something obscure, with a geometric pattern. The candles burned. One spluttered, turned itself out. C fell asleep. D drank wine until the bottle was finished. D put down the book and left C alone. C woke up then fell. D came in to draw the curtains and blow out the remaining candles. D loved the smell and the look of the smoke. The electric light was on and D turned that off too. D took away the bottle and glasses. C could be seen by the light of the moon. As C awoke, the night turned and the hoo-hooing began again.

CHAPTER 47

In the living room: windows big, to let through the right light, the pictures where they needed to be and the chairs hard and comfortable. At 9 o'clock D came into the room, sat down and began to read the book that was on the old table. C offered D a glass of wine. D accepted. C poured. Silence. An occasional glance up around the room. Candles flickered. C offered D another glass which D declined. D put down the book, got up, left C alone. Now C sighed. Outside, the sound of the evening wood was heard. The sound of the wood. C poured out more wine and picked up the paper and pen that had been bought as a present. C would write to S. How to begin? It had been so long. It was tricky. The pen and paper down again. D entered again and C had fallen asleep. Would D like more wine? Yes, this time. D put on the pullover. It was not cold inside. C thought how D looked and how the pullover looked too. They both read their books. C's book was a novel. D was reading something obscure, with a geometric pattern. The candles burned. One spluttered, turned itself out. C fell asleep. D drank wine until the bottle was finished. D put down the book and left C alone. C woke up then fell. D came in to draw the curtains and blow out the remaining candles. D loved the smell and the look of the smoke. The electric light was on and D turned that off too. D took away the bottle and glasses. C could be seen by the light of the moon. As C awoke, the night turned and the hoo-hooing began again.

CHAPTER 48

In the living room: windows big, to let through the right light, the pictures where they needed to be and the chairs hard and comfortable. At 9 o'clock D came into the room, sat down and began to read the book that was on the old table. C offered D a glass of wine. D accepted. C poured. Silence. An occasional glance up around the room. Candles flickered. C offered D another glass which D declined. D put down the book, got up, left C alone. Now C sighed. Outside, the sound of the evening wood was heard. The sound of the. C poured out more wine and picked up the paper and pen that had been bought as a present. C would write to S. How to begin? It had been so long. It was tricky. The pen and paper down again. D entered again and C had fallen asleep. Would D like more wine? Yes, this time. D put on the pullover. It was not cold inside. C thought how D looked and how the pullover looked too. They both read their books. C's book was a novel. D was reading something obscure, with a geometric pattern. The candles burned. One spluttered, turned itself out. C fell asleep. D drank wine until the bottle was finished. D put down the book and left C alone. C woke up then fell. D came in to draw the curtains and blow out the remaining candles. D loved the smell and the look of the smoke. The electric light was on and D turned that off too. D took away the bottle and glasses. C could be seen by the light of the moon. As C awoke, the night turned and the hoo-hooing began again.

CHAPTER 49

In the living room: windows big, to let through the right light, the pictures where they needed to be and the chairs hard and comfortable. At 9 o'clock D came into the room, sat down and began to read the book that was on the old table. C offered D a glass of wine. D accepted. C poured. Silence. An occasional glance up around the room. Candles flickered. C offered D another glass which D declined. D put down the book, got up, left C alone. Now C sighed. Outside, the sound of the evening wood was heard. Of the. C poured out more wine and picked up the paper and pen that had been bought as a present. C would write to S. How to begin? It had been so long. It was tricky. The pen and paper down again. D entered again and C had fallen asleep. Would D like more wine? Yes, this time. D put on the pullover. It was not cold inside. C thought how D looked and how the pullover looked too. They both read their books. C's book was a novel. D was reading something obscure, with a geometric pattern. The candles burned. One spluttered, turned itself out. C fell asleep. D drank wine until the bottle was finished. D put down the book and left C alone. C woke up then fell. D came in to draw the curtains and blow out the remaining candles. D loved the smell and the look of the smoke. The electric light was on and D turned that off too. D took away the bottle and glasses. C could be seen by the light of the moon. As C awoke, the night turned and the hoo-hooing began again.

CHAPTER 50

In the living room: windows big, to let through the right light, the pictures where they needed to be and the chairs comfortable. At 9 o'clock D came into the room, sat down and began to read the book that was on the old table. C offered D a glass of wine. D accepted. C poured. Silence. An occasional glance up around the room. Candles flickered. C offered D another glass which D declined. D put down the book, got up, left C alone. Now C sighed. Outside, the sound of the evening wood was heard. Of the. C poured out more wine and picked up the paper and pen that had been bought as a present. C would write to S. How to begin? It had been so long. It was tricky. The pen and paper down again. D entered again and C had fallen asleep. Would D like more wine? Yes, this time. D put on the pullover. It was not cold inside. C thought how D looked and how the pullover looked too. They both read their books. C's book was a novel. D was reading something obscure, with a geometric pattern. The candles burned. One spluttered, turned itself out. C fell asleep. D drank wine until the bottle was finished. D put down the book and left C alone. C woke up then fell. D came in to draw the curtains and blow out the remaining candles. D loved the smell and the look of the smoke. The electric light was on and D turned that off too. D took away the bottle and glasses. C could be seen by the light of the moon. As C awoke, the night turned and the hoo-hooing began again.

CHAPTER 51

In the living room: windows big, to let through the right light, the pictures where they needed to be and the chairs comfortable. At 9 o'clock D came into the room, sat down and began to read the book that was on the old table. C offered D a glass of wine. D accepted. C poured. Silence. An occasional glance up around the room. Candles flickered. C offered D another glass which D declined. D put down the book, got up, left C alone. Now C sighed. Outside, the sound of the evening wood was heard. Of the. C poured out more wine and picked up the paper and pen that had been bought as a present. C would write to S. How to begin? It had been so long. It was tricky. The pen and paper down again. D entered again and C had fallen asleep. Would D like more wine? Yes, this time. D put on the pullover. It was not cold inside. C thought how D looked and how the pullover looked too. They both read their books. C's book was a novel. D was reading something obscure, with a geometric pattern. The candles burned. One spluttered, turned itself out. C fell. D drank wine until the bottle was finished. D put down the book and left C alone. C woke up then fell. D came in to draw the curtains and blow out the remaining candles. D loved the smell and the look of the smoke. The electric light was on and D turned that off too. D took away the bottle and glasses. C could be seen by the light of the moon. As C awoke, the night turned and the hoo-hooing began again.

CHAPTER 52

The living room: windows big, to let through the right light, the pictures where they needed to be and the chairs comfortable. At 9 o'clock D came into the room, sat down and began to read the book that was on the old table. C offered D a glass of wine. D accepted. C poured. Silence. An occasional glance up around the room. Candles flickered. C offered D another glass which D declined. D put down the book, got up, left C alone. Now C sighed. Outside, the sound of the evening wood was heard. Of the. C poured out more wine and picked up the paper and pen that had been bought as a present. C would write to S. How to begin? It had been so long. It was tricky. The pen and paper down again. D entered again and C had fallen asleep. Would D like more wine? Yes, this time. D put on the pullover. It was not cold inside. C thought how D looked and how the pullover looked too. They both read their books. C's book was a novel. D was reading something obscure, with a geometric pattern. The candles burned. One spluttered, turned itself out. C fell. D drank wine until the bottle was finished. D put down the book and left C alone. C woke up then fell. D came in to draw the curtains and blow out the remaining candles. D loved the smell and the look of the smoke. The electric light was on and D turned that off too. D took away the bottle and glasses. C could be seen by the light of the moon. As C awoke, the night turned and the hoo-hooing began again.

CHAPTER 53

The living room: windows big, to let through the right light, the pictures where they needed to be and the chairs comfortable. At 9 o'clock D came into the room, sat and began to read the book that was on the old table. C offered D a glass of wine. D accepted. C poured. Silence. An occasional glance up around the room. Candles flickered. C offered D another glass which D declined. D put down the book, got up, left C alone. Now C sighed. Outside, the sound of the evening wood was heard. Of the. C poured out more wine and picked up the paper and pen that had been bought as a present. C would write to S. How to begin? It had been so long. It was tricky. The pen and paper down again. D entered again and C had fallen asleep. Would D like more wine? Yes, this time. D put on the pullover. It was not cold inside. C thought how D looked and how the pullover looked too. They both read their books. C's book was a novel. D was reading something obscure, with a geometric pattern. The candles burned. One spluttered, turned itself out. C fell. D drank wine until the bottle was finished. D put down the book and left C alone. C woke up then fell. D came in to draw the curtains and blow out the remaining candles. D loved the smell and the look of the smoke. The electric light was on and D turned that off too. D took away the bottle and glasses. C could be seen by the light of the moon. As C awoke, the night turned and the hoo-hooing began again.

CHAPTER 54

The living room: windows big, to let through the light, the pictures where they needed to be and the chairs comfortable. At 9 o'clock D came into the room, sat and began to read the book that was on the old table. C offered D a glass of wine. D accepted. C poured. Silence. An occasional glance up around the room. Candles flickered. C offered D another glass which D declined. D put down the book, got up, left C alone. Now C sighed. Outside, the sound of the evening wood was heard. Of the. C poured out more wine and picked up the paper and pen that had been bought as a present. C would write to S. How to begin? It had been so long. It was tricky. The pen and paper down again. D entered again and C had fallen asleep. Would D like more wine? Yes, this time. D put on the pullover. It was not cold inside. C thought how D looked and how the pullover looked too. They both read their books. C's book was a novel. D was reading something obscure, with a geometric pattern. The candles burned. One spluttered, turned itself out. C fell. D drank wine until the bottle was finished. D put down the book and left C alone. C woke up then fell. D came in to draw the curtains and blow out the remaining candles. D loved the smell and the look of the smoke. The electric light was on and D turned that off too. D took away the bottle and glasses. C could be seen by the light of the moon. As C awoke, the night turned and the hoo-hooing began again.

CHAPTER 55

The living room: windows big, to let through the light, the pictures where they needed to be and the chairs comfortable. At 9 o'clock D came into the room, sat and began to read the book that was on the old table. C offered D a glass of wine. D accepted. C poured. Silence. An occasional glance up around the room. Candles flickered. C offered D another glass which D declined. D put down the book, got up, left C alone. Now C sighed. Outside, the sound of the evening wood was heard. Of. C poured out more wine and picked up the paper and pen that had been bought as a present. C would write to S. How to begin? It had been so long. It was tricky. The pen and paper down again. D entered again and C had fallen asleep. Would D like more wine? Yes, this time. D put on the pullover. It was not cold inside. C thought how D looked and how the pullover looked too. They both read their books. C's book was a novel. D was reading something obscure, with a geometric pattern. The candles burned. One spluttered, turned itself out. C fell. D drank wine until the bottle was finished. D put down the book and left C alone. C woke up then fell. D came in to draw the curtains and blow out the remaining candles. D loved the smell and the look of the smoke. The electric light was on and D turned that off too. D took away the bottle and glasses. C could be seen by the light of the moon. As C awoke, the night turned and the hoo-hooing began again.

CHAPTER 56

The living room: windows big, to let through the light, the pictures where they needed to be and the chairs comfortable. At 9 o'clock D came into the room, sat and began to read the book that was on the old table. C offered D a glass of wine. D accepted. C poured. Silence. An occasional glance up around the room. Candles flickered. C offered D another glass which D declined. D put down the book, got up, left C alone. Now C sighed. Outside, the sound of the evening wood was heard. C poured out more wine and picked up the paper and pen that had been bought as a present. C would write to S. How to begin? It had been so long. It was tricky. The pen and paper down again. D entered again and C had fallen asleep. Would D like more wine? Yes, this time. D put on the pullover. It was not cold inside. C thought how D looked and how the pullover looked too. They both read their books. C's book was a novel. D was reading something obscure, with a geometric pattern. The candles burned. One spluttered, turned itself out. C fell. D drank wine until the bottle was finished. D put down the book and left C alone. C woke up then fell. D came in to draw the curtains and blow out the remaining candles. D loved the smell and the look of the smoke. The electric light was on and D turned that off too. D took away the bottle and glasses. C could be seen by the light of the moon. As C awoke, the night turned and the hoo-hooing began again.

CHAPTER 57

The living room: windows big, to let through the light, the pictures where they needed to be and the chairs comfortable. At 9 o'clock D came into the room, sat and began to read the book that was on the old table. C offered D a glass of wine. D accepted. C poured. Silence. An occasional glance up around the room. Candles flickered. C offered D another glass which D declined. D put down the book, got up, left C alone. Now C sighed. Outside, the sound of the evening wood was heard. C poured out more wine and picked up the paper and pen that had been bought as a present. C would write to S. How to begin? It had been so long. It was tricky. The pen and paper down again. D entered again and C had fallen asleep. Would D like more wine? Yes, this time. D put on the pullover. It was not cold inside. C thought how D looked and how the pullover looked too. They both read their books. C's book was a novel. D was reading something with a geometric pattern. The candles burned. One spluttered, turned itself out. C fell. D drank wine until the bottle was finished. D put down the book and left C alone. C woke up then fell. D came in to draw the curtains and blow out the remaining candles. D loved the smell and the look of the smoke. The electric light was on and D turned that off too. D took away the bottle and glasses. C could be seen by the light of the moon. As C awoke, the night turned and the hoo-hooing began again.

CHAPTER 58

The living room: windows big to let through the light, the pictures where they needed to be and the chairs comfortable. At 9 o'clock D came into the room, sat and began to read the book that was on the old table. C offered D a glass of wine. D accepted. C poured. Silence. An occasional glance up around the room. Candles flickered. C offered D another glass which D declined. D put down the book, got up, left C alone. Now C sighed. Outside, the sound of the evening wood was heard. C poured out more wine and picked up the paper and pen that had been bought as a present. C would write to S. How to begin? It had been so long. It was tricky. The pen and paper down again. D entered again and C had fallen asleep. Would D like more wine? Yes, this time. D put on the pullover. It was not cold inside. C thought how D looked and how the pullover looked too. They both read their books. C's book was a novel. D was reading something with a geometric pattern. The candles burned. One spluttered, turned itself out. C fell. D drank wine until the bottle was finished, put down the book and left C alone. C woke up then fell. D came in to draw the curtains and blow out the remaining candles. D loved the smell and the look of the smoke. The electric light was on and D turned that off too. D took away the bottle and glasses. C could be seen by the light of the moon. As C awoke, the night turned and the hoo-hooing began again.

CHAPTER 59

The living room: windows big to let through the light, the pictures where they needed to be and the chairs comfortable. At 9 o'clock D came into the room, sat and began to read the book that was on the old table. C offered D a glass of wine. D accepted. C poured. Silence. An occasional glance up around the room. Candles flickered. C offered D another glass which D declined. D put down the book, got up, left C alone. Now C sighed. Outside, the sound of the evening wood was heard. C poured out more wine and picked up the paper and pen that had been bought as a present. C would write to S. How to begin? It had been so long. It was tricky. The pen and paper down. D entered again and C had fallen asleep. Would D like more wine? Yes, this time. D put on the pullover. It was not cold inside. C thought how D looked and how the pullover looked too. They both read their books. C's book was a novel. D was reading something with a geometric pattern. The candles burned. One spluttered, turned itself out. C fell. D drank wine until the bottle was finished, put down the book and left C alone. C woke up then fell. D came in to draw the curtains and blow out the remaining candles. D loved the smell and the look of the smoke. The electric light was on and D turned that off too. D took away the bottle and glasses. C could be seen by the light of the moon. As C awoke, the night turned and the hoo-hooing began again.

CHAPTER 60

The living room: windows big to let through the light, the pictures where they needed to be and the chairs comfortable. At 9 o'clock D came into the room, sat and began to read the book that was on the old table. C offered D a glass of wine. D accepted. C poured. Silence. An occasional glance up around the room. Candles flickered. C offered D another glass which D declined. D put down the book, got up, left C alone. Now C sighed. Outside, the sound of the evening wood was heard. C poured out more wine and picked up the paper and pen that had been bought as a present. C would write to S. How to begin? It had been so long. It was tricky. The pen and paper down. D entered again and C had fallen asleep. Would D like more wine? Yes, this time. D put on the pullover. It was not cold inside. C thought how D looked and how the pullover looked too. They both read their books. C's book was a novel. D was reading something with a geometric pattern. The candles burned. One spluttered, turned itself out. C fell. D drank wine until the bottle was finished, put down the book and left C alone. C woke up then fell. D came in to draw the curtains and blow out the remaining candles. D loved the smell and the look of the smoke. The electric light was on and D turned that off too. D took away the bottle and glasses. The light of the moon. As C awoke, the night turned and the hoo-hooing began again.

CHAPTER 61

The living room: windows big to let through the light, the pictures where they needed to be and the chairs comfortable. At 9 o'clock D came into the room, sat and began to read the book that was on the old table. C offered D a glass of wine. D accepted. C poured. Silence. An occasional glance up around the room. Candles flickered. C offered D another glass which D declined. D put down the book, got up, left C alone. Now C sighed. Outside, the sound of the evening wood was heard. C poured out more wine and picked up the paper and pen that had been bought as a present. C would write to S. How to begin? It had been so long. It was tricky. The pen and paper down. D entered again and C had fallen asleep. Would D like more wine? Yes, this time. D put on the pullover. It was not cold inside. C thought how D looked and how the pullover looked too. They both read their books. C's book was a novel. D was reading something with a geometric pattern. The candles burned. One spluttered, turned itself out. C fell. D drank wine until the bottle was finished, put down the book and left C alone. C woke up then fell. D came in to draw the curtains and blow out the remaining candles. D loved the smell and the look of the smoke. The electric light was on and D turned that off too. D took away the bottle and glasses. The light. The moon. As C awoke, the night turned and the hoo-hooing began again.

CHAPTER 62

The living room: windows big, let through the light, the pictures where they needed to be and the chairs comfortable. At 9 o'clock D came into the room, sat and began to read the book that was on the old table. C offered D a glass of wine. D accepted. C poured. Silence. An occasional glance up around the room. Candles flickered. C offered D another glass which D declined. D put down the book, got up, left C alone. Now C sighed. Outside, the sound of the evening wood was heard. C poured out more wine and picked up the paper and pen that had been bought as a present. C would write to S. How to begin? It had been so long. It was tricky. The pen and paper down. D entered again and C had fallen asleep. Would D like more wine? Yes, this time. D put on the pullover. It was not cold inside. C thought how D looked and how the pullover looked too. They both read their books. C's book was a novel. D was reading something with a geometric pattern. The candles burned. One spluttered, turned itself out. C fell. D drank wine until the bottle was finished, put down the book and left C alone. C woke up then fell. D came in to draw the curtains and blow out the remaining candles. D loved the smell and the look of the smoke. The electric light was on and D turned that off too. D took away the bottle and glasses. The light. The moon. As C awoke, the night turned and the hoo-hooing began again.

CHAPTER 63

The living room: windows big, let through the light, the pictures where they needed to be and the chairs comfortable. At 9 o'clock D came into the room, sat and began to read the book that was on the old table. C offered D a glass of wine. D accepted. C poured. Silence. An occasional glance up around the room. Candles flickered. C offered D another glass which D declined. D put down the book, got up, left C alone. Now C sighed. Outside, the sound of the evening wood was heard. C poured out more wine and picked up the paper and pen that had been bought as a present. C would write to S. How to begin? It had been so long. It was tricky. The pen and paper down. D entered again: C had fallen asleep. Would D like more wine? Yes, this time. D put on the pullover. It was not cold inside. C thought how D looked and how the pullover looked too. They both read their books. C's book was a novel. D was reading something with a geometric pattern. The candles burned. One spluttered, turned itself out. C fell. D drank wine until the bottle was finished, put down the book and left C alone. C woke up then fell. D came in to draw the curtains and blow out the remaining candles. D loved the smell and the look of the smoke. The electric light was on and D turned that off too. D took away the bottle and glasses. The light. The moon. As C awoke, the night turned and the hoo-hooing began again.

CHAPTER 64

The living room: windows big, let through the light, the pictures where they needed to be and the chairs comfortable. At 9 o'clock D came into the room, sat and began to read the book that was on the old table. C offered D a glass of wine. D accepted. C poured. Silence. An occasional glance up around the room. Candles flickered. C offered D another glass which D declined. D put down the book, got up, left C alone. Now C sighed. Outside, the sound of the evening wood was heard. C poured out more wine and picked up the paper and pen that had been bought as a present. C would write to S. How to begin? It had been so long. It was tricky. The pen and paper down. D entered again: C had fallen asleep. Would D like more wine? Yes, this time. D put on the pullover. It was not cold inside. C thought how D looked and how the pullover looked too. They both read their books. C's book was a novel. D was reading something with a geometric pattern. The candles burned. One spluttered, turned itself out. C fell. D drank wine until the bottle was finished, put down the book and left C alone. C woke up then fell. D came in to draw the curtains and blow out the remaining candles. D loved the smell, the look of the smoke. The electric light was on and D turned that off too. D took away the bottle and glasses. The light. The moon. As C awoke, the night turned and the hoo-hooing began again.

CHAPTER 65

The living room: windows let through the light, the pictures where they needed to be and the chairs comfortable. At 9 o'clock D came into the room, sat and began to read the book that was on the old table. C offered D a glass of wine. D accepted. C poured. Silence. An occasional glance up around the room. Candles flickered. C offered D another glass which D declined. D put down the book, got up, left C alone. Now C sighed. Outside, the sound of the evening wood was heard. C poured out more wine and picked up the paper and pen that had been bought as a present. C would write to S. How to begin? It had been so long. It was tricky. The pen and paper down. D entered again: C had fallen asleep. Would D like more wine? Yes, this time. D put on the pullover. It was not cold inside. C thought how D looked and how the pullover looked too. They both read their books. C's book was a novel. D was reading something with a geometric pattern. The candles burned. One spluttered, turned itself out. C fell. D drank wine until the bottle was finished, put down the book and left C alone. C woke up then fell. D came in to draw the curtains and blow out the remaining candles. D loved the smell, the look of the smoke. The electric light was on and D turned that off too. D took away the bottle and glasses. The light. The moon. As C awoke, the night turned and the hoo-hooing began again.

CHAPTER 66

The room: windows let through the light, the pictures where they needed to be and the chairs comfortable. At 9 o'clock D came into the room, sat and began to read the book that was on the old table. C offered D a glass of wine. D accepted. C poured. Silence. An occasional glance up around the room. Candles flickered. C offered D another glass which D declined. D put down the book, got up, left C alone. Now C sighed. Outside, the sound of the evening wood was heard. C poured out more wine and picked up the paper and pen that had been bought as a present. C would write to S. How to begin? It had been so long. It was tricky. The pen and paper down. D entered again: C had fallen asleep. Would D like more wine? Yes, this time. D put on the pullover. It was not cold inside. C thought how D looked and how the pullover looked too. They both read their books. C's book was a novel. D was reading something with a geometric pattern. The candles burned. One spluttered, turned itself out. C fell. D drank wine until the bottle was finished, put down the book and left C alone. C woke up then fell. D came in to draw the curtains and blow out the remaining candles. D loved the smell, the look of the smoke. The electric light was on and D turned that off too. D took away the bottle and glasses. The light. The moon. As C awoke, the night turned and the hoo-hooing began again.

CHAPTER 67

The room: windows let through the light, the pictures where they needed to be and the chairs comfortable. At 9 o'clock D came into the room, sat and began to read the book that was on the old table. C offered D a glass of wine. D accepted. C poured. An occasional glance up around the room. Candles flickered. C offered D another glass which D declined. D put down the book, got up, left C alone. Now C sighed. Outside, the sound of the evening wood was heard. C poured out more wine and picked up the paper and pen that had been bought as a present. C would write to S. How to begin? It had been so long. It was tricky. The pen and paper down. D entered again: C had fallen asleep. Would D like more wine? Yes, this time. D put on the pullover. It was not cold inside. C thought how D looked and how the pullover looked too. They both read their books. C's book was a novel. D was reading something with a geometric pattern. The candles burned. One spluttered, turned itself out. C fell. D drank wine until the bottle was finished, put down the book and left C alone. C woke up then fell. D came in to draw the curtains and blow out the remaining candles. D loved the smell, the look of the smoke. The electric light was on and D turned that off too. D took away the bottle and glasses. The light. The moon. As C awoke, the night turned and the hoo-hooing began again.

CHAPTER 68

The room: windows let through the light, the pictures where they needed to be and the chairs comfortable. At 9 o'clock D came in, sat and began to read the book that was on the old table. C offered D a glass of wine. D accepted. C poured. An occasional glance up around the room. Candles flickered. C offered D another glass which D declined. D put down the book, got up, left C alone. Now C sighed. Outside, the sound of the evening wood was heard. C poured out more wine and picked up the paper and pen that had been bought as a present. C would write to S. How to begin? It had been so long. It was tricky. The pen and paper down. D entered again: C had fallen asleep. Would D like more wine? Yes, this time. D put on the pullover. It was not cold inside. C thought how D looked and how the pullover looked too. They both read their books. C's book was a novel. D was reading something with a geometric pattern. The candles burned. One spluttered, turned itself out. C fell. D drank wine until the bottle was finished, put down the book and left C alone. C woke up then fell. D came in to draw the curtains and blow out the remaining candles. D loved the smell, the look of the smoke. The electric light was on and D turned that off too. D took away the bottle and glasses. The light. The moon. As C awoke, the night turned and the hoo-hooing began again.

CHAPTER 69

The room: windows let through the light, the pictures where they needed to be and the chairs comfortable. At 9 o'clock D came in, sat and began to read the book that was on the old table. C offered D a glass of wine. D accepted. C poured. An occasional glance up around the room. Candles flickered. C offered D another glass which D declined. D put down the book, got up, left C alone. Now C sighed. Outside, the sound of the evening wood was heard. C poured out more wine and picked up the paper and pen that had been bought as a present. C would write to S. How to begin? It had been so long. It was tricky. The pen and paper down. D entered again: C had fallen asleep. Would D like more wine? Yes, this time. D put on the pullover. It was not cold inside. C thought how D looked and how the pullover looked too. They both read their books. C's book was a novel. D was reading something with a geometric pattern. The candles burned. One spluttered, turned itself out. D drank wine until the bottle was finished, put down the book and left C alone. C woke up then fell. D came in to draw the curtains and blow out the remaining candles. D loved the smell, the look of the smoke. The electric light was on and D turned that off too. D took away the bottle and glasses. The light. The moon. As C awoke, the night turned and the hoo-hooing began again.

CHAPTER 70

The room: windows let through the light, the pictures where they needed to be and the chairs comfortable. At 9 o'clock D came in, sat and began to read the book that was on the old table. C offered D a glass of wine. D accepted. C poured. An occasional glance up around the room. Candles flickered. C offered D another glass which D declined. D put down the book, got up, left C alone. Now C sighed. Outside, the sound of the evening wood was heard. C poured out more wine and picked up the paper and pen that had been bought as a present. C would write to S. How to begin? It had been so long. It was tricky. The pen and paper down. D entered again: C had fallen asleep. Would D like more wine? Yes, this time. D put on the pullover. It was not cold inside. C thought how D looked and how the pullover looked too. They both read their books. C's book was a novel. D was reading something with a geometric pattern. The candles burned. One spluttered, turned itself out. D drank wine until the bottle was finished, put down the book and left C alone. C woke up then fell. D came in to draw the curtains and blow out the remaining candles. D loved the smell, the look of the smoke. The electric light was on and D turned that off too. D took away the bottle. The light. The moon. As C awoke, the night turned and the hoo-hooing began again.

CHAPTER 71

Windows let through the light, the pictures where they needed to be and the chairs comfortable. At 9 o'clock D came in, sat and began to read the book that was on the old table. C offered D a glass of wine. D accepted. C poured. An occasional glance up around the room. Candles flickered. C offered D another glass which D declined. D put down the book, got up, left C alone. Now C sighed. Outside, the sound of the evening wood was heard. C poured out more wine and picked up the paper and pen that had been bought as a present. C would write to S. How to begin? It had been so long. It was tricky. The pen and paper down. D entered again: C had fallen asleep. Would D like more wine? Yes, this time. D put on the pullover. It was not cold inside. C thought how D looked and how the pullover looked too. They both read their books. C's book was a novel. D was reading something with a geometric pattern. The candles burned. One spluttered, turned itself out. D drank wine until the bottle was finished, put down the book and left C alone. C woke up then fell. D came in to draw the curtains and blow out the remaining candles. D loved the smell, the look of the smoke. The electric light was on and D turned that off too. D took away the bottle. The light moon. As C awoke, the night turned and the hoo-hooing began again.

CHAPTER 72

Windows let through the light, the pictures where they needed to be and the chairs comfortable. At 9 o'clock D came in, sat and began to read the book that was on the old table. C offered D a glass of wine. D accepted. C poured. An occasional glance up around the room. Candles flickered. C offered D another glass which D declined. D put down the book, got up, left C alone. Now C sighed. Outside, the sound of the evening wood was heard. C poured out more wine and picked up the paper and pen that had been bought as a present. C would write to S. How? It had been so long. It was tricky. The pen and paper down. D entered again: C had fallen asleep. Would D like more wine? Yes, this time. D put on the pullover. It was not cold inside. C thought how D looked and how the pullover looked too. They both read their books. C's book was a novel. D was reading something with a geometric pattern. The candles burned. One spluttered, turned itself out. D drank wine until the bottle was finished, put down the book and left C alone. C woke up then fell. D came in to draw the curtains and blow out the remaining candles. D loved the smell, the look of the smoke. The electric light was on and D turned that off too. D took away the bottle. The light moon. As C awoke, the night turned and the hoo-hooing began again.

CHAPTER 73

Windows let through the light, the pictures where they needed to be and the chairs comfortable. At 9 o'clock D came in, sat and began to read the book that was on the old table. C offered D a glass of wine. D accepted. C poured. An occasional glance up around the room. Candles flickered. C offered D another glass which D declined. D put down the book, got up, left C alone. Now C sighed. Outside, the sound of the evening wood was heard. C poured out more wine and picked up the paper and pen that had been bought as a present. C would write to S. How? It had been so long. It was tricky. The pen and paper down. D entered again: C had fallen asleep. Would D like more wine? Yes. D put on the pullover. It was not cold inside. C thought how D looked and how the pullover looked too. They both read their books. C's book was a novel. D was reading something with a geometric pattern. The candles burned. One spluttered, turned itself out. D drank wine until the bottle was finished, put down the book and left C alone. C woke up then fell. D came in to draw the curtains and blow out the remaining candles. D loved the smell, the look of the smoke. The electric light was on and D turned that off too. D took away the bottle. The light moon. As C awoke, the night turned and the hoo-hooing began again.

CHAPTER 74

Windows let through the light, the pictures where they needed to be and the chairs comfortable. At 9 o'clock D came in, sat and began to read the book that was on the old table. C offered D a glass of wine. D accepted. C poured. An occasional glance up around the room. Candles flickered. C offered D another glass which D declined. D put down the book, got up, left C alone. Now C sighed. Outside, the sound of the evening wood was heard. C poured out more wine and picked up the paper and pen that had been bought as a present. C would write to S. How? It had been so long. It was tricky. The pen and paper down. D entered again: C had fallen asleep. Would D like more wine? Yes. D put on the pullover. It was not cold inside. C thought how D looked, how the pullover looked too. They both read their books. C's book was a novel. D was reading something with a geometric pattern. The candles burned. One spluttered, turned itself out. D drank wine until the bottle was finished, put down the book and left C alone. C woke up then fell. D came in to draw the curtains and blow out the remaining candles. D loved the smell, the look of the smoke. The electric light was on and D turned that off too. D took away the bottle. The light moon. As C awoke, the night turned and the hoo-hooing began again.

CHAPTER 75

Windows let through the light, the pictures where they needed to be and the chairs comfortable. At 9 o'clock D came in, sat and began to read the book that was on the old table. C offered D a glass of wine. D accepted. C poured. An occasional glance up around the room. Candles flickered. C offered D another glass which D declined. D put down the book, got up, left C alone. Now C sighed. Outside, the sound of the evening wood was heard. C poured out more wine and picked up the paper and pen that had been bought as a present. C would write to S. How? It had been so long. It was tricky. The pen and paper down. D entered again: C had fallen asleep. Would D like more wine? Yes. D put on the pullover. It was not cold inside. C thought how D looked, how the pullover looked too. They both read their books. C's book was a novel. D was reading something with a geometric pattern. The candles burned. One spluttered, turned itself out. D drank wine until the bottle was finished, put down the book and left C alone. C woke up then fell. D came in to draw the curtains and blow out the remaining candles. D loved the smell of the smoke. The electric light was on and D turned that off too. D took away the bottle. The light moon. As C awoke, the night turned and the hoo-hooing began again.

CHAPTER 76

Windows let through the light, the pictures where they needed to be and the chairs comfortable. At 9 o'clock D came in, sat and began to read the book that was on the old table. C offered D a glass of wine. D accepted. C poured. An occasional glance up around the room. Candles flickered. C offered D another glass which D declined. D put down the book, got up, left C alone. Now C sighed. Outside, the sound of the evening wood was heard. C poured out more wine and picked up the paper and pen that had been bought as a present. C would write to S. It had been so long. It was tricky. The pen and paper down. D entered again: C had fallen asleep. Would D like more wine? Yes. D put on the pullover. It was not cold inside. C thought how D looked, how the pullover looked too. They both read their books. C's book was a novel. D was reading something with a geometric pattern. The candles burned. One spluttered, turned itself out. D drank wine until the bottle was finished, put down the book and left C alone. C woke up then fell. D came in to draw the curtains and blow out the remaining candles. D loved the smell of the smoke. The electric light was on and D turned that off too. D took away the bottle. The light moon. As C awoke, the night turned and the hoo-hooing began again.

CHAPTER 77

Windows let through the light, the pictures where they needed to be and the chairs comfortable. At 9 o'clock D came in, sat and began to read the book that was on the old table. C offered D a glass of wine. D accepted. C poured. An occasional glance up around the room. Candles flickered. C offered D another glass which D declined. D put down the book, got up, left C alone. Now C sighed. Outside, the sound of the evening wood was heard. C poured out more wine and picked up the paper and pen that had been bought as a present. C would write to S. It had been so long. It was tricky. The pen and paper down. D entered again: C had fallen asleep. Would D like more wine? Yes. D put on the pullover. It was not cold inside. C thought how D looked, how the pullover looked too. They both read their books. C's book was a novel. D was reading something with a pattern. The candles burned. One spluttered, turned itself out. D drank wine until the bottle was finished, put down the book and left C alone. C woke up then fell. D came in to draw the curtains and blow out the remaining candles. D loved the smell of the smoke. The electric light was on and D turned that off too. D took away the bottle. The light moon. As C awoke, the night turned and the hoo-hooing began again.

CHAPTER 78

Windows let through the light, the pictures where they needed to be and the chairs comfortable. At 9 o'clock D came in, sat and began to read the book that was on the old table. C offered D a glass of wine. D accepted. C poured. An occasional glance up around the room. Candles flickered. C offered D another glass which D declined. D put down the book, got up, left C alone. Now C sighed. Outside, the sound of the evening wood was heard. C poured out more wine and picked up the paper and pen that had been bought as a present. C would write to S. It had been so long. It was tricky. The pen and paper down. D entered again: C had fallen asleep. Would D like more wine? Yes. D put on the pullover. It was not cold inside. C thought how D looked, how the pullover looked too. They both read their books. C's book was a novel. D was reading something with a pattern. The candles burned. One spluttered, turned itself out. D drank wine until the bottle was finished and left C alone. C woke up then fell. D came in to draw the curtains and blow out the remaining candles. D loved the smell of the smoke. The electric light was on and D turned that off too. D took away the bottle. The light moon. As C awoke, the night turned and the hoo-hooing began again.

CHAPTER 79

Windows let through the light, the pictures where they needed to be and the chairs comfortable. At 9 o'clock D came in, sat and began to read the book that was on the old table. C offered D a glass of wine. D accepted. C poured. An occasional glance up around the room. Candles flickered. C offered D another glass which D declined. D put down the book, got up, left C alone. Now C sighed. Outside, the sound of the evening wood was heard. C poured out more wine and picked up the paper and pen that had been bought as a present. C would write to S. It had been so long. It was tricky. The pen and paper down. D entered again: C had fallen asleep. Would D like more wine? Yes. D put on the pullover. It was not cold inside. C thought how D looked, how the pullover looked too. They both read their books. C's book was a novel. D was reading something with a pattern. Candles burned. One spluttered, turned itself out. D drank wine until the bottle was finished and left C alone. C woke up then fell. D came in to draw the curtains and blow out the remaining candles. D loved the smell of the smoke. The electric light was on and D turned that off too. D took away the bottle. The light moon. As C awoke, the night turned and the hoo-hooing began again.

CHAPTER 80

Windows let through the light, where they needed to be. And the chairs comfortable. At 9 o'clock D came in, sat and began to read the book that was on the old table. C offered D a glass of wine. D accepted. C poured. An occasional glance up around the room. Candles flickered. C offered D another glass which D declined. D put down the book, got up, left C alone. Now C sighed. Outside, the sound of the evening wood was heard. C poured out more wine and picked up the paper and pen that had been bought as a present. C would write to S. It had been so long. It was tricky. The pen and paper down. D entered again: C had fallen asleep. Would D like more wine? Yes. D put on the pullover. It was not cold inside. C thought how D looked, how the pullover looked too. They both read their books. C's book was a novel. D was reading something with a pattern. Candles burned. One spluttered, turned itself out. D drank wine until the bottle was finished and left C alone. C woke up then fell. D came in to draw the curtains and blow out the remaining candles. D loved the smell of the smoke. The electric light was on and D turned that off too. D took away the bottle. The light moon. As C awoke, the night turned and the hoo-hooing began again.

CHAPTER 81

Windows let through the light, where they needed to be. And the chairs comfortable. At 9 o'clock D came in, sat and began to read the book that was on the old table. C offered D a glass of wine. D accepted. C poured. An occasional glance up around the room. Candles flickered. C offered D another glass which D declined. D put down the book, got up, left C alone. Now C sighed. Outside, the sound of the evening wood was heard. C poured out more wine and picked up the paper and pen that had been bought as a present. C would write to S. It had been so long. It was tricky. The pen down. D entered again: C had fallen asleep. Would D like more wine? Yes. D put on the pullover. It was not cold inside. C thought how D looked, how the pullover looked too. They both read their books. C's book was a novel. D was reading something with a pattern. Candles burned. One spluttered, turned itself out. D drank wine until the bottle was finished and left C alone. C woke up then fell. D came in to draw the curtains and blow out the remaining candles. D loved the smell of the smoke. The electric light was on and D turned that off too. D took away the bottle. The light moon. As C awoke, the night turned and the hoo-hooing began again.

CHAPTER 82

Windows let through the light, where they needed to be. And the chairs comfortable. At 9 o'clock D came in, sat and began to read the book that was on the old table. C offered D a glass of wine. D accepted. C poured. An occasional glance up around the room. Candles flickered. C offered D another glass which D declined. D put down the book, got up, left C alone. Now C sighed. Outside, the sound of the evening wood. C poured out more wine and picked up the paper and pen that had been bought as a present. C would write to S. It had been so long. It was tricky. The pen down. D entered again: C had fallen asleep. Would D like more wine? Yes. D put on the pullover. It was not cold inside. C thought how D looked, how the pullover looked too. They both read their books. C's book was a novel. D was reading something with a pattern. Candles burned. One spluttered, turned itself out. D drank wine until the bottle was finished and left C alone. C woke up then fell. D came in to draw the curtains and blow out the remaining candles. D loved the smell of the smoke. The electric light was on and D turned that off too. D took away the bottle. The light moon. As C awoke, the night turned and the hoo-hooing began again.

CHAPTER 83

Windows let through the light, they needed to. And the chairs comfortable. At 9 o'clock D came in, sat and began to read the book that was on the old table. C offered D a glass of wine. D accepted. C poured. An occasional glance up around the room. Candles flickered. C offered D another glass which D declined. D put down the book, got up, left C alone. Now C sighed. Outside, the sound of the evening wood. C poured out more wine and picked up the paper and pen that had been bought as a present. C would write to S. It had been so long. It was tricky. The pen down. D entered again: C had fallen asleep. Would D like more wine? Yes. D put on the pullover. It was not cold inside. C thought how D looked, how the pullover looked too. They both read their books. C's book was a novel. D was reading something with a pattern. Candles burned. One spluttered, turned itself out. D drank wine until the bottle was finished and left C alone. C woke up then fell. D came in to draw the curtains and blow out the remaining candles. D loved the smell of the smoke. The electric light was on and D turned that off too. D took away the bottle. The light moon. As C awoke, the night turned and the hoo-hooing began again.

CHAPTER 84

Windows let through the light, they needed to. And the chairs comfortable. At 9 o'clock D came in, sat and began to read the book that was on the old table. C offered D a glass of wine. D accepted. C poured. An occasional glance up around the room. Candles flickered. C offered D another glass which D declined. D put down the book, got up, left C alone. Now C sighed. Outside, the sound of the evening wood. C poured out more wine and picked up the paper and pen that had been bought as a present. C would write to S. It had been so long. It was tricky. The pen down. D entered again: C had fallen asleep. Would D like more wine? Yes. D put on the pullover. It was not cold inside. C thought how D looked, how the pullover looked. They both read their books. C's book was a novel. D was reading something with a pattern. Candles burned. One spluttered, turned itself out. D drank wine until the bottle was finished and left C alone. C woke up then fell. D came in to draw the curtains and blow out the remaining candles. D loved the smell of the smoke. The electric light was on and D turned that off too. D took away the bottle. The light moon. As C awoke, the night turned and the hoo-hooing began again.

CHAPTER 85

Windows let through the light, they needed to. And the chairs comfortable. At 9 o'clock D came in and began to read the book that was on the old table. C offered D a glass of wine. D accepted. C poured. An occasional glance up around the room. Candles flickered. C offered D another glass which D declined. D put down the book, got up, left C alone. Now C sighed. Outside, the sound of the evening wood. C poured out more wine and picked up the paper and pen that had been bought as a present. C would write to S. It had been so long. It was tricky. The pen down. D entered again: C had fallen asleep. Would D like more wine? Yes. D put on the pullover. It was not cold inside. C thought how D looked, how the pullover looked. They both read their books. C's book was a novel. D was reading something with a pattern. Candles burned. One spluttered, turned itself out. D drank wine until the bottle was finished and left C alone. C woke up then fell. D came in to draw the curtains and blow out the remaining candles. D loved the smell of the smoke. The electric light was on and D turned that off too. D took away the bottle. The light moon. As C awoke, the night turned and the hoo-hooing began again.

CHAPTER 86

Windows let through the light, they needed to. And the chairs comfortable. At 9 o'clock D came in and began to read the book that was on the old table. C offered D a glass of wine. C poured. An occasional glance up around the room. Candles flickered. C offered D another glass which D declined. D put down the book, got up, left C alone. Now C sighed. Outside, the sound of the evening wood. C poured out more wine and picked up the paper and pen that had been bought as a present. C would write to S. It had been so long. It was tricky. The pen down. D entered again: C had fallen asleep. Would D like more wine? Yes. D put on the pullover. It was not cold inside. C thought how D looked, how the pullover looked. They both read their books. C's book was a novel. D was reading something with a pattern. Candles burned. One spluttered, turned itself out. D drank wine until the bottle was finished and left C alone. C woke up then fell. D came in to draw the curtains and blow out the remaining candles. D loved the smell of the smoke. The electric light was on and D turned that off too. D took away the bottle. The light moon. As C awoke, the night turned and the hoo-hooing began again.

CHAPTER 87

Windows let through the light and the chairs comfortable. At 9 o'clock D came in and began to read the book that was on the old table. C offered D a glass of wine. C poured. An occasional glance up around the room. Candles flickered. C offered D another glass which D declined. D put down the book, got up, left C alone. Now C sighed. Outside, the sound of the evening wood. C poured out more wine and picked up the paper and pen that had been bought as a present. C would write to S. It had been so long. It was tricky. The pen down. D entered again: C had fallen asleep. Would D like more wine? Yes. D put on the pullover. It was not cold inside. C thought how D looked, how the pullover looked. They both read their books. C's book was a novel. D was reading something with a pattern. Candles burned. One spluttered, turned itself out. D drank wine until the bottle was finished and left C alone. C woke up then fell. D came in to draw the curtains and blow out the remaining candles. D loved the smell of the smoke. The electric light was on and D turned that off too. D took away the bottle. The light moon. As C awoke, the night turned and the hoo-hooing began again.

CHAPTER 88

Windows let through the light and the chairs comfortable. At 9 o'clock D came in and began to read the book that was on the old table. C offered D a glass of wine. C poured. An occasional glance up around the room. Candles flickered. C offered D another glass which D declined. D put down the book, got up, left C alone. Now C sighed. Outside, the sound of the evening wood. C poured out more wine and picked up the paper and pen that had been bought as a present. C would write to S. It had been so long. It was tricky. The pen down. D entered again: C had fallen asleep. Would D like more wine? Yes. D put on the pullover. It was not cold inside. C thought how D looked, how the pullover looked. They both read their books. C's book was a novel. D was reading something with a pattern. Candles burned. One spluttered itself out. D drank wine until the bottle was finished and left C alone. C woke up then fell. D came in to draw the curtains and blow out the remaining candles. D loved the smell of the smoke. The electric light was on and D turned that off too. D took away the bottle. The light moon. As C awoke, the night turned and the hoo-hooing began again.

CHAPTER 89

Windows let through the light and the chairs comfortable. At 9 o'clock D came in and began to read the book that was on the old table. C offered D wine. C poured. An occasional glance up around the room. Candles flickered. C offered D another glass which D declined. D put down the book, got up, left C alone. Now C sighed. Outside, the sound of the evening wood. C poured out more wine and picked up the paper and pen that had been bought as a present. C would write to S. It had been so long. It was tricky. The pen down. D entered again: C had fallen asleep. Would D like more wine? Yes. D put on the pullover. It was not cold inside. C thought how D looked, how the pullover looked. They both read their books. C's book was a novel. D was reading something with a pattern. Candles burned. One spluttered itself out. D drank wine until the bottle was finished and left C alone. C woke up then fell. D came in to draw the curtains and blow out the remaining candles. D loved the smell of the smoke. The electric light was on and D turned that off too. D took away the bottle. The light moon. As C awoke, the night turned and the hoo-hooing began again.

CHAPTER 90

Windows let through the light and the chairs comfortable. At 9 o'clock D came in and began to read the book that was on the old table. C offered D wine. C poured. An occasional glance around the room. Candles flickered. C offered D another glass which D declined. D put down the book, got up, left C alone. Now C sighed. Outside, the sound of the evening wood. C poured out more wine and picked up the paper and pen that had been bought as a present. C would write to S. It had been so long. It was tricky. The pen down. D entered again: C had fallen asleep. Would D like more wine? Yes. D put on the pullover. It was not cold inside. C thought how D looked, how the pullover looked. They both read their books. C's book was a novel. D was reading something with a pattern. Candles burned. One spluttered itself out. D drank wine until the bottle was finished and left C alone. C woke up then fell. D came in to draw the curtains and blow out the remaining candles. D loved the smell of the smoke. The electric light was on and D turned that off too. D took away the bottle. The light moon. As C awoke, the night turned and the hoo-hooing began again.

CHAPTER 91

Windows let through the light and the chairs comfortable. At 9 o'clock D came in and began to read the book that was on the old table. C offered D wine. C poured. A glance around the room. Candles flickered. C offered D another glass which D declined. D put down the book, got up, left C alone. Now C sighed. Outside, the sound of the evening wood. C poured out more wine and picked up the paper and pen that had been bought as a present. C would write to S. It had been so long. It was tricky. The pen down. D entered again: C had fallen asleep. Would D like more wine? Yes. D put on the pullover. It was not cold inside. C thought how D looked, how the pullover looked. They both read their books. C's book was a novel. D was reading something with a pattern. Candles burned. One spluttered itself out. D drank wine until the bottle was finished and left C alone. C woke up then fell. D came in to draw the curtains and blow out the remaining candles. D loved the smell of the smoke. The electric light was on and D turned that off too. D took away the bottle. The light moon. As C awoke, the night turned and the hoo-hooing began again.

CHAPTER 92

Windows let through the light and the chairs comfortable. At 9 o'clock D came in and began to read the book that was on the old table. C offered D wine. C poured. A glance around the room. Candles flickered. C offered D another glass which D declined. D put down the book, got up, left C alone. Now C sighed. Outside, the sound of the evening wood. C poured out more wine and picked up the paper and pen that had been bought as a present. C would write to S. It had been so long. It was tricky. The pen down. D entered again: C had fallen asleep. Would D like more wine? Yes. D put on the pullover. It was not cold inside. C thought how D looked, how the pullover looked. They both read their books. C's book was a novel. D was reading something with a pattern. Candles burned. One spluttered itself out. D drank wine until the bottle was finished and left C alone. C woke up then fell. D came in to draw the curtains and blow out the remaining candles. D loved the smell of the smoke. The electric light was on and D turned that off too. D took away the bottle. The light. As C awoke, the night turned and the hoo-hooing began again.

CHAPTER 93

Windows let through the light and the chairs comfortable. At 9 o'clock D came in and began to read the book that was on the old table. C offered D wine. C poured. A glance around the room. Candles. C offered D another glass which D declined. D put down the book, got up, left C alone. Now C sighed. Outside, the sound of the evening wood. C poured out more wine and picked up the paper and pen that had been bought as a present. C would write to S. It had been so long. It was tricky. The pen down. D entered again: C had fallen asleep. Would D like more wine? Yes. D put on the pullover. It was not cold inside. C thought how D looked, how the pullover looked. They both read their books. C's book was a novel. D was reading something with a pattern. Candles burned. One spluttered itself out. D drank wine until the bottle was finished and left C alone. C woke up then fell. D came in to draw the curtains and blow out the remaining candles. D loved the smell of the smoke. The electric light was on and D turned that off too. D took away the bottle. The light. As C awoke, the night turned and the hoo-hooing began again.

CHAPTER 94

Windows let through the light and the chairs comfortable. At 9 o'clock D came in and began to read the book that was on the old table. C offered D wine. C poured. A glance around the room. Candles. C offered D another glass which D declined. D put down the book, got up, left C alone. Now C sighed. Outside, the sound of the evening wood. C poured out more wine and picked up the paper and pen that had been bought as a present. C would write to S. It had been so long. It was tricky. The pen down. D entered again: C had fallen asleep. Would D like more wine? Yes. D put on the pullover. It was not cold inside. C thought how D looked, how the pullover looked. They both read. C's book was a novel. D was reading something with a pattern. Candles burned. One spluttered itself out. D drank wine until the bottle was finished and left C alone. C woke up then fell. D came in to draw the curtains and blow out the remaining candles. D loved the smell of the smoke. The electric light was on and D turned that off too. D took away the bottle. The light. As C awoke, the night turned and the hoo-hooing began again.

CHAPTER 95

Windows let through the light, the chairs comfortable. At 9 o'clock D came in and began to read the book that was on the old table. C offered D wine. C poured. A glance around the room. Candles. C offered D another glass which D declined. D put down the book, got up, left C alone. Now C sighed. Outside, the sound of the evening wood. C poured out more wine and picked up the paper and pen that had been bought as a present. C would write to S. It had been so long. It was tricky. The pen down. D entered again: C had fallen asleep. Would D like more wine? Yes. D put on the pullover. It was not cold inside. C thought how D looked, how the pullover looked. They both read. C's book was a novel. D was reading something with a pattern. Candles burned. One spluttered itself out. D drank wine until the bottle was finished and left C alone. C woke up then fell. D came in to draw the curtains and blow out the remaining candles. D loved the smell of the smoke. The electric light was on and D turned that off too. D took away the bottle. The light. As C awoke, the night turned and the hoo-hooing began again.

CHAPTER 96

Windows let through the light, the chairs comfortable. At 9 o'clock D came in and began to read the book that was on the old table. C offered D wine. C poured. A glance around the room. Candles. C offered D another glass. D declined. D put down the book, got up, left C alone. Now C sighed. Outside, the sound of the evening wood. C poured out more wine and picked up the paper and pen that had been bought as a present. C would write to S. It had been so long. It was tricky. The pen down. D entered again: C had fallen asleep. Would D like more wine? Yes. D put on the pullover. It was not cold inside. C thought how D looked, how the pullover looked. They both read. C's book was a novel. D was reading something with a pattern. Candles burned. One spluttered itself out. D drank wine until the bottle was finished and left C alone. C woke up then fell. D came in to draw the curtains and blow out the remaining candles. D loved the smell of the smoke. The electric light was on and D turned that off too. D took away the bottle. The light. As C awoke, the night turned and the hoo-hooing began again.

CHAPTER 97

Windows let through the light, the chairs comfortable. At 9 o'clock D came in and began to read the book that was on the old table. C offered D wine. C poured. A glance around the room. Candles. C offered D another glass. D declined. D put down the book, got up, left C alone. Now C sighed. Outside, the sound of the evening wood. C poured out more wine and picked up the paper and pen that had been bought as a present. C would write to S. It had been so long. It was tricky. The pen down. D entered again: C had fallen asleep. Would D like more wine? Yes. D put on the pullover. It was not cold inside. C thought how D looked, how the pullover looked. They both read. C's book was a novel. D was reading something with a pattern. Candles burned. One spluttered itself out. D drank wine until the bottle was finished and left C alone. C woke up then fell. D came in to draw the curtains and blow out the remaining candles. D loved the smell of the smoke. The electric light was on and D turned that off too. D took away the bottle. Light. As C awoke, the night turned and the hoo-hooing began again.

CHAPTER 98

Windows let through the light, the chairs comfortable. At 9 o'clock D came in and began to read the book that was on the old table. C offered D wine. C poured. A glance around the room. Candles. C offered D another glass. D declined. D put down the book, got up, left C alone. Now C sighed. Outside, the sound of the evening wood. C poured out more wine and picked up the paper and pen that had been bought as a present. C would write to S. It had been so long. It was tricky. The pen down. D entered again: C had fallen asleep. Would D like more wine? Yes. D put on the pullover. It was not cold inside. C thought how the pullover looked. They both read. C's book was a novel. D was reading something with a pattern. Candles burned. One spluttered itself out. D drank wine until the bottle was finished and left C alone. C woke up then fell. D came in to draw the curtains and blow out the remaining candles. D loved the smell of the smoke. The electric light was on and D turned that off too. D took away the bottle. Light. As C awoke, the night turned and the hoo-hooing began again.

CHAPTER 99

Windows let through the light, the chairs comfortable. At 9 o'clock D came in and began to read the book that was on the old table. C offered D wine. C poured. A glance around the room. Candles. C offered D another glass. D declined. D put down the book, got up, left C alone. Now C sighed. Outside, the sound of the evening wood. C poured out more wine and picked up the paper and pen that had been bought as a present. C would write to S. It had been so long. It was tricky. The pen down. D entered again: C had fallen asleep. Would D like more wine? Yes. D put on the pullover. It was not cold inside. C thought how the pullover looked. They both read. C's book was a novel. D was reading something with a pattern. Candles burned. One spluttered itself out. D drank wine until the bottle was finished and left C alone. C woke up then fell. D came in to draw the curtains and blow out the remaining candles. D loved the smell of the smoke. The electric light was on and D turned that off too. D took away the bottle. As C awoke, the night turned and the hoo-hooing began again.

CHAPTER 100

Windows let through the light, the chairs comfortable. At 9 o'clock D came in and began to read the book that was on the table. C offered D wine. C poured. A glance around the room. Candles. C offered D another glass. D declined. D put down the book, got up, left C alone. Now C sighed. Outside, the sound of the evening wood. C poured out more wine and picked up the paper and pen that had been bought as a present. C would write to S. It had been so long. It was tricky. The pen down. D entered again: C had fallen asleep. Would D like more wine? Yes. D put on the pullover. It was not cold inside. C thought how the pullover looked. They both read. C's book was a novel. D was reading something with a pattern. Candles burned. One spluttered itself out. D drank wine until the bottle was finished and left C alone. C woke up then fell. D came in to draw the curtains and blow out the remaining candles. D loved the smell of the smoke. The electric light was on and D turned that off too. D took away the bottle. As C awoke, the night turned and the hoo-hooing began again.

CHAPTER 101

Windows let through the light, the chairs comfortable. At 9 o'clock D came in and began to read the book that was on the table. C offered D wine. C poured. A glance around the room. Candles. C offered D another glass. D declined. D put down the book, got up, left C alone. Now C sighed. Outside, the sound of the evening wood. C poured out more wine and picked up the paper and pen that had been bought as a present. C would write to S. It had been so long. It was tricky. The pen down. D entered again: C had fallen. Would D like more wine? Yes. D put on the pullover. It was not cold inside. C thought how the pullover looked. They both read. C's book was a novel. D was reading something with a pattern. Candles burned. One spluttered itself out. D drank wine until the bottle was finished and left C alone. C woke up then fell. D came in to draw the curtains and blow out the remaining candles. D loved the smell of the smoke. The electric light was on and D turned that off too. D took away the bottle. As C awoke, the night turned and the hoo-hooing began again.

CHAPTER 102

Windows let through the light, the chairs comfortable. At 9 o'clock D came in and began to read the book that was on the table. C offered D wine. C poured. A glance around the room. Candles. C offered D another glass. D declined. D put down the book, got up, left C alone. Now C sighed. Outside, the sound of the wood. C poured out more wine and picked up the paper and pen that had been bought as a present. C would write to S. It had been so long. It was tricky. The pen down. D entered again: C had fallen. Would D like more wine? Yes. D put on the pullover. It was not cold inside. C thought how the pullover looked. They both read. C's book was a novel. D was reading something with a pattern. Candles burned. One spluttered itself out. D drank wine until the bottle was finished and left C alone. C woke up then fell. D came in to draw the curtains and blow out the remaining candles. D loved the smell of the smoke. The electric light was on and D turned that off too. D took away the bottle. As C awoke, the night turned and the hoo-hooing began again.

CHAPTER 103

Windows let through the light, the chairs comfortable. At 9 o'clock D came in and began to read the book that was on the table. C offered D wine. C poured. A glance around the room. Candles. C offered D another glass. D declined. D put down the book, got up, left C alone. Now C sighed. Outside, the sound of the wood. C poured out more wine and picked up the paper and pen that had been bought as a present. C would write to S. It was tricky. The pen down. D entered again: C had fallen. Would D like more wine? Yes. D put on the pullover. It was not cold inside. C thought how the pullover looked. They both read. C's book was a novel. D was reading something with a pattern. Candles burned. One spluttered itself out. D drank wine until the bottle was finished and left C alone. C woke up then fell. D came in to draw the curtains and blow out the remaining candles. D loved the smell of the smoke. The electric light was on and D turned that off too. D took away the bottle. As C awoke, the night turned and the hoo-hooing began again.

CHAPTER 104

Windows let through the light, the chairs comfortable. At 9 o'clock D came in and began to read the book that was on the table. C offered D wine. C poured. A glance around the room. Candles. C offered D another glass. D declined. D put down the book, got up, left C alone. Now C sighed. Outside, the sound of the wood. C poured out more wine and picked up the paper and pen that had been bought as a present. C would write to S. It was tricky. The pen down. D entered again: C had fallen. Would D like more wine? Yes. D put on the pullover. It was not cold. C thought how the pullover looked. They both read. C's book was a novel. D was reading something with a pattern. Candles burned. One spluttered itself out. D drank wine until the bottle was finished and left C alone. C woke up then fell. D came in to draw the curtains and blow out the remaining candles. D loved the smell of the smoke. The electric light was on and D turned that off too. D took away the bottle. As C awoke, the night turned and the hoo-hooing began again.

CHAPTER 105

Windows let through the light, the chairs comfortable. At 9 o'clock D came in and began to read the book that was on the table. C offered D wine. C poured. A glance around the room. Candles. C offered D another glass. D declined. D put down the book, left C alone. Now C sighed. Outside, the sound of the wood. C poured out more wine and picked up the paper and pen that had been bought as a present. C would write to S. It was tricky. The pen down. D entered again: C had fallen. Would D like more wine? Yes. D put on the pullover. It was not cold. C thought how the pullover looked. They both read. C's book was a novel. D was reading something with a pattern. Candles burned. One spluttered itself out. D drank wine until the bottle was finished and left C alone. C woke up then fell. D came in to draw the curtains and blow out the remaining candles. D loved the smell of the smoke. The electric light was on and D turned that off too. D took away the bottle. As C awoke, the night turned and the hoo-hooing began again.

CHAPTER 106

Windows let through the light, the chairs comfortable. At 9 o'clock D came in and began to read the book that was on the table. C offered D wine. C poured. A glance around the room. Candles. C offered D another glass. D declined. D put down the book, left C alone. Now C sighed. Outside, the sound of the wood. C poured out more wine and picked up the paper and pen that had been bought as a present. C would write to S. It was tricky. The pen down. D entered again: C had fallen. Would D like more wine? Yes. D put on the pullover. It was not cold. C thought how the pullover looked. They both read. C's book was a novel, D's something with a pattern. Candles burned. One spluttered itself out. D drank wine until the bottle was finished and left C alone. C woke up then fell. D came in to draw the curtains and blow out the remaining candles. D loved the smell of the smoke. The electric light was on and D turned that off too. D took away the bottle. As C awoke, the night turned and the hoo-hooing began again.

CHAPTER 107

Windows let through the light, the chairs comfortable. At 9 o'clock D came in and began to read the book that was on the table. C offered D wine. C poured. A glance around the room. Candles. C offered D another glass. D declined. D put down the book, left C alone. Now C sighed. Outside, the sound of the wood. C poured out more wine and picked up the paper and pen that had been bought as a present. C would write to S. It was tricky. The pen down. D entered again: C had fallen. Would D like more wine? Yes. D put on the pullover. It was not cold. C thought how the pullover looked. They both read. C's book was a novel, D's something with a pattern. Candles burned. One spluttered itself out. D drank wine until the bottle was finished and left C alone. C woke then fell. D came in to draw the curtains and blow out the remaining candles. D loved the smell of the smoke. The electric light was on and D turned that off too. D took away the bottle. As C awoke, the night turned and the hoo-hooing began again.

CHAPTER 108

Windows let through the light, the chairs comfortable. At 9 o'clock D came in and began to read the book that was on the table. C offered D wine. C poured. A glance around the room. Candles. C offered D another glass. D declined. D put down the book, left C alone. Now C sighed. Outside, the sound of the wood. C poured out more wine and picked up the paper and pen that had been bought as a present. C would write to S. It was tricky. The pen down. D entered again: C had fallen. Would D like more wine? Yes. D put on the pullover. It was not cold. C thought how the pullover looked. They both read. C's book was a novel, D's something with a pattern. Candles burned. One spluttered itself out. D drank wine until the bottle was finished and left C alone. C woke then fell. D came in to draw the curtains and blow out the remaining candles. D loved the smell. The electric light was on and D turned that off too. D took away the bottle. As C awoke, the night turned and the hoo-hooing began again.

CHAPTER 109

Windows let through the light, the chairs comfortable. At 9 o'clock D came in and began to read the book that was on the table. C offered D wine. C poured. A glance around the room. Candles. C offered D another glass. D declined. D put down the book, left C alone. Now C sighed. Outside, the sound of the wood. C poured out more wine and picked up the paper and pen that had been bought as a present. C would write to S. It was tricky. The pen down. D entered again: C had fallen. Would D like more wine? Yes. D put on the pullover. It was not cold. C thought how the pullover looked. They both read. C's was a novel, D's something with a pattern. Candles burned. One spluttered itself out. D drank wine until the bottle was finished and left C alone. C woke then fell. D came in to draw the curtains and blow out the remaining candles. D loved the smell. The electric light was on and D turned that off too. D took away the bottle. As C awoke, the night turned and the hoo-hooing began again.

CHAPTER 110

Windows let through the light, the chairs comfortable. At 9 o'clock D came in and began to read the book that was on the table. C offered D wine. C poured. A glance around the room. Candles. C offered D another glass. D declined. D put down the book, left C alone. Now C sighed. Outside, the sound of the wood. C poured out more wine and picked up the paper and pen that had been bought as a present. C would write to S. It was tricky. The pen down. D entered again: C had fallen. Would D like more wine? Yes. D put on the pullover. It was not cold. C thought how the pullover looked. They both read. C's was a novel, D's something with a pattern. Candles burned. One spluttered itself out. D drank wine until the bottle was finished and left C alone. C woke then fell. D came in to draw the curtains and blow out the remaining candles. D loved the smell. The electric light was on, D turned that off too. D took away the bottle. As C awoke, the night turned and the hoo-hooing began again.

CHAPTER 111

Windows let through the light, the chairs comfortable. At 9 o'clock D came in and began to read the book that was on the table. C offered D wine. C poured. A glance around the room. Candles. C offered D another glass. D declined. D put down the book, left C alone. Now C sighed. Outside, the sound of the wood. C poured out more wine and picked up the paper and pen that had been bought as a present. C would write to S. Tricky. The pen down. D entered again: C had fallen. Would D like more wine? Yes. D put on the pullover. It was not cold. C thought how the pullover looked. They both read. C's was a novel, D's something with a pattern. Candles burned. One spluttered itself out. D drank wine until the bottle was finished and left C alone. C woke then fell. D came in to draw the curtains and blow out the remaining candles. D loved the smell. The electric light was on, D turned that off too. D took away the bottle. As C awoke, the night turned and the hoo-hooing began again.

CHAPTER 112

Windows let through the light, the chairs comfortable. At 9 o'clock D came in and began to read the book that was on the table. C offered D wine. C poured. A glance around the room. Candles. C offered D another glass. D declined. D put down the book, left C alone. Now C sighed. Outside, the sound of the wood. C poured out more wine and picked up the paper and pen that had been bought as a present. C would write to S. Tricky. The pen down. D entered again: C had fallen. Would D like more wine? Yes. D put on the pullover. It was not cold. C thought how the pullover looked. They both read. C's was a novel, D's something with a pattern. Candles burned. One spluttered out. D drank wine until the bottle was finished and left C alone. C woke then fell. D came in to draw the curtains and blow out the remaining candles. D loved the smell. The electric light was on, D turned that off too. D took away the bottle. As C awoke, the night turned and the hoo-hooing began again.

CHAPTER 113

Windows let through the light, the chairs comfortable. At 9 o'clock D came in and began to read the book that was on the table. C offered D wine. C poured. A glance around the room. Candles. C offered D another glass. D declined. D put down the book, left C alone. Now C sighed. Outside, the sound of the wood. C poured out more wine and picked up the paper and pen that had been bought as a present. C would write to S. Tricky. The pen down. D entered again: C had fallen. Would D like more wine? Yes. D put on the pullover. It was not cold. C thought how the pullover looked. They both read. C's was a novel, D's something with a pattern. Candles burned. One spluttered out. D drank wine until the bottle was finished and left C alone. C then fell. D came in to draw the curtains and blow out the remaining candles. D loved the smell. The electric light was on, D turned that off too. D took away the bottle. As C awoke, the night turned and the hoo-hooing began again.

CHAPTER 114

Windows let through the light, the chairs comfortable. At 9 o'clock D came in and began to read the book that was on the table. C offered D wine. C poured. A glance around the room. Candles. C offered D another glass. D declined. D put down the book, left C alone. Now C sighed. Outside, the sound of the wood. C poured out more wine and picked up the paper and pen that had been bought as a present. C would write to S. Tricky. The pen down. D entered again: C had fallen. Would D like more wine? Yes. D put on the pullover. It was not cold. C thought how the pullover looked. They both read. C's was a novel, D's something with a pattern. Candles burned. One spluttered out. D drank wine until the bottle was finished and left C alone. C then fell. D came in to draw the curtains and blow out the remaining candles. D loved the smell. The electric light was on, D turned that off too. D took the bottle. As C awoke, the night turned and the hoo-hooing began again.

CHAPTER 115

Windows let through the light, the chairs comfortable. At 9 o'clock D came in and began to read the book on the table. C offered D wine. C poured. A glance around the room. Candles. C offered D another glass. D declined. D put down the book, left C alone. Now C sighed. Outside, the sound of the wood. C poured out more wine and picked up the paper and pen that had been bought as a present. C would write to S. Tricky. The pen down. D entered again: C had fallen. Would D like more wine? Yes. D put on the pullover. It was not cold. C thought how the pullover looked. They both read. C's was a novel, D's something with a pattern. Candles burned. One spluttered out. D drank wine until the bottle was finished and left C alone. C then fell. D came in to draw the curtains and blow out the remaining candles. D loved the smell. The electric light was on, D turned that off too. D took the bottle. As C awoke, the night turned and the hoo-hooing began again.

CHAPTER 116

Windows let through the light, the chairs comfortable. At 9 o'clock D came in and began to read the book on the table. C offered D wine. C poured. A glance around. Candles. C offered D another glass. D declined. D put down the book, left C alone. Now C sighed. Outside, the sound of the wood. C poured out more wine and picked up the paper and pen that had been bought as a present. C would write to S. Tricky. The pen down. D entered again: C had fallen. Would D like more wine? Yes. D put on the pullover. It was not cold. C thought how the pullover looked. They both read. C's was a novel, D's something with a pattern. Candles burned. One spluttered out. D drank wine until the bottle was finished and left C alone. C then fell. D came in to draw the curtains and blow out the remaining candles. D loved the smell. The electric light was on, D turned that off too. D took the bottle. As C awoke, the night turned and the hoo-hooing began again.

CHAPTER 117

Windows let through the light, the chairs comfortable. At 9 o'clock D came in and began to read the book on the table. C offered D wine. C poured. A glance around. C offered D another glass. D declined. D put down the book, left C alone. Now C sighed. Outside, the sound of the wood. C poured out more wine and picked up the paper and pen that had been bought as a present. C would write to S. Tricky. The pen down. D entered again: C had fallen. Would D like more wine? Yes. D put on the pullover. It was not cold. C thought how the pullover looked. They both read. C's was a novel, D's something with a pattern. Candles burned. One spluttered out. D drank wine until the bottle was finished and left C alone. C then fell. D came in to draw the curtains and blow out the remaining candles. D loved the smell. The electric light was on, D turned that off too. D took the bottle. As C awoke, the night turned and the hoo-hooing began again.

CHAPTER 118

Windows let through the light, the chairs comfortable. At 9 o'clock D came in and began to read the book on the table. C offered D wine. C poured. A glance around. C offered D another glass. D declined. D put down the book, left C alone. Now C sighed. Outside, the sound of the wood. C poured out more wine and picked up the paper and pen that had been bought as a present. C would write to S. Tricky. The pen down. D entered again: C had fallen. Would D like more wine? Yes. D put on the pullover. It was not cold. C thought how the pullover looked. They both read. C's was a novel, D's something with a pattern. Candles burned. One spluttered out. D drank wine until the bottle was finished and left C alone. C fell. D came in to draw the curtains and blow out the remaining candles. D loved the smell. The electric light was on, D turned that off too. D took the bottle. As C awoke, the night turned and the hoo-hooing began again.

CHAPTER 119

Windows, the light, the chairs comfortable. At 9 o'clock D came in and began to read the book on the table. C offered D wine. C poured. A glance around. C offered D another glass. D declined. D put down the book, left C alone. Now C sighed. Outside, the sound of the wood. C poured out more wine and picked up the paper and pen that had been bought as a present. C would write to S. Tricky. The pen down. D entered again: C had fallen. Would D like more wine? Yes. D put on the pullover. It was not cold. C thought how the pullover looked. They both read. C's was a novel, D's something with a pattern. Candles burned. One spluttered out. D drank wine until the bottle was finished and left C alone. C fell. D came in to draw the curtains and blow out the remaining candles. D loved the smell. The electric light was on, D turned that off too. D took the bottle. As C awoke, the night turned and the hoo-hooing began again.

CHAPTER 120

The light, the chairs comfortable. At 9 o'clock D came in and began to read the book on the table. C offered D wine. C poured. A glance around. C offered D another glass. D declined. D put down the book, left C alone. Now C sighed. Outside, the sound of the wood. C poured out more wine and picked up the paper and pen that had been bought as a present. C would write to S. Tricky. The pen down. D entered again: C had fallen. Would D like more wine? Yes. D put on the pullover. It was not cold. C thought how the pullover looked. They both read. C's was a novel, D's something with a pattern. Candles burned. One spluttered out. D drank wine until the bottle was finished and left C alone. C fell. D came in to draw the curtains and blow out the remaining candles. D loved the smell. The electric light was on, D turned that off too. D took the bottle. As C awoke, the night turned and the hoo-hooing began again.

CHAPTER 121

The light, the chairs comfortable. At 9 o'clock D came in and began to read the book on the table. C offered D wine. C poured. A glance around. C offered D another glass. D declined. D put down the book, left C alone. Now C sighed. Outside, the sound of the wood. C poured out more wine and picked up the paper and pen that had been bought as a present. C would write to S. The pen down. D entered again: C had fallen. Would D like more wine? Yes. D put on the pullover. It was not cold. C thought how the pullover looked. They both read. C's was a novel, D's something with a pattern. Candles burned. One spluttered out. D drank wine until the bottle was finished and left C alone. C fell. D came in to draw the curtains and blow out the remaining candles. D loved the smell. The electric light was on, D turned that off too. D took the bottle. As C awoke, the night turned and the hoo-hooing began again.

CHAPTER 122

Light, the chairs comfortable. At 9 o'clock D came in and began to read the book on the table. C offered D wine. C poured. A glance around. C offered D another glass. D declined. D put down the book, left C alone. Now C sighed. Outside, the sound of the wood. C poured out more wine and picked up the paper and pen that had been bought as a present. C would write to S. The pen down. D entered again: C had fallen. Would D like more wine? Yes. D put on the pullover. It was not cold. C thought how the pullover looked. They both read. C's was a novel, D's something with a pattern. Candles burned. One spluttered out. D drank wine until the bottle was finished and left C alone. C fell. D came in to draw the curtains and blow out the remaining candles. D loved the smell. The electric light was on, D turned that off too. D took the bottle. As C awoke, the night turned and the hoo-hooing began again.

CHAPTER 123

Light, the chairs comfortable. At 9 o'clock D came in and began to read the book on the table. C offered D wine. A glance around. C offered D another glass. D declined. D put down the book, left C alone. Now C sighed. Outside, the sound of the wood. C poured out more wine and picked up the paper and pen that had been bought as a present. C would write to S. The pen down. D entered again: C had fallen. Would D like more wine? Yes. D put on the pullover. It was not cold. C thought how the pullover looked. They both read. C's was a novel, D's something with a pattern. Candles burned. One spluttered out. D drank wine until the bottle was finished and left C alone. C fell. D came in to draw the curtains and blow out the remaining candles. D loved the smell. The electric light was on, D turned that off too. D took the bottle. As C awoke, the night turned and the hoo-hooing began again.

CHAPTER 124

Light, the chairs comfortable. At 9 o'clock D came in and began to read the book on the table. C offered D wine. A glance around. C offered D another glass. D declined. D put down the book, left C alone. Now C sighed. Outside, the sound of the wood. C poured out more wine and picked up the paper and pen that had been bought as a present. C would write to S. The pen down. D entered again: C had fallen. Would D like more wine? Yes. D put on the pullover. It was not cold. C thought how the pullover looked. They both read. C's was a novel, something with a pattern. Candles burned. One spluttered out. D drank wine until the bottle was finished and left C alone. C fell. D came in to draw the curtains and blow out the remaining candles. D loved the smell. The electric light was on, D turned that off too. D took the bottle. As C awoke, the night turned and the hoo-hooing began again.

CHAPTER 125

Light, the chairs comfortable. At 9 o'clock D came in and began to read the book on the table. C offered D wine. A glance around. C offered D another glass. D declined. D put down the book, left C alone. Now C sighed. Outside, the sound of the wood. C poured out more wine and picked up the paper and pen that had been bought as a present. C would write to S. The pen down. D entered again: C had fallen. Would D like more wine? Yes. D put on the pullover. It was not cold. C thought how the pullover looked. They both read. C's was a novel, something with a pattern. Candles burned. One spluttered out. D drank wine until the bottle was finished and left C alone. C fell. D came in to draw the curtains and blow out the remaining candles. D loved the smell. The electric light was on, D turned that off too. D took the bottle. As C awoke, night turned and the hoo-hooing began again.

CHAPTER 126

Light, the chairs comfortable. At 9 o'clock D came in and began to read the book on the table. C offered D wine. A glance around. C offered D another glass. D declined. D put down the book, left C alone. Now C sighed. Outside, the sound of the wood. C poured out more wine and picked up the paper and pen that had been bought as a present. C would write to S. The pen down. D entered again: C had fallen. Would D like more wine? Yes. D put on the pullover. It was cold. C thought how the pullover looked. They both read. C's was a novel, something with a pattern. Candles burned. One spluttered out. D drank wine until the bottle was finished and left C alone. C fell. D came in to draw the curtains and blow out the remaining candles. D loved the smell. The electric light was on, D turned that off too. D took the bottle. As C awoke, night turned and the hoo-hooing began again.

CHAPTER 127

The chairs comfortable. At 9 o'clock D came in and began to read the book on the table. C offered D wine. A glance around. C offered D another glass. D declined. D put down the book, left C alone. Now C sighed. Outside, the sound of the wood. C poured out more wine and picked up the paper and pen that had been bought as a present. C would write to S. The pen down. D entered again: C had fallen. Would D like more wine? Yes. D put on the pullover. It was cold. C thought how the pullover looked. They both read. C's was a novel, something with a pattern. Candles burned. One spluttered out. D drank wine until the bottle was finished and left C alone. C fell. D came in to draw the curtains and blow out the remaining candles. D loved the smell. The electric light was on, D turned that off too. D took the bottle. As C awoke, night turned and the hoo-hooing began again.

CHAPTER 128

The chairs comfortable. At 9 o'clock D came in and began to read the book on the table. C offered D wine. A glance around. C offered D another glass. D declined, put down the book, left C alone. Now C sighed. Outside, the sound of the wood. C poured out more wine and picked up the paper and pen that had been bought as a present. C would write to S. The pen down. D entered again: C had fallen. Would D like more wine? Yes. D put on the pullover. It was cold. C thought how the pullover looked. They both read. C's was a novel, something with a pattern. Candles burned. One spluttered out. D drank wine until the bottle was finished and left C alone. C fell. D came in to draw the curtains and blow out the remaining candles. D loved the smell. The electric light was on, D turned that off too. D took the bottle. As C awoke, night turned and the hoo-hooing began again.

CHAPTER 129

The chairs comfortable. At 9 o'clock D came in and began to read the book on the table. C offered D wine. A glance around. C offered D another glass. D declined, put down the book, left C alone. Now C sighed. Outside, the sound of the wood. C poured out more wine and picked up the paper and pen that had been bought as a present. C would write to S. D entered again: C had fallen. Would D like more wine? Yes. D put on the pullover. It was cold. C thought how the pullover looked. They both read. C's was a novel, something with a pattern. Candles burned. One spluttered out. D drank wine until the bottle was finished and left C alone. C fell. D came in to draw the curtains and blow out the remaining candles. D loved the smell. The electric light was on, D turned that off too. D took the bottle. As C awoke, night turned and the hoo-hooing began again.

CHAPTER 130

The chairs comfortable. At 9 o'clock D came in and began to read the book on the table. C offered D wine. A glance around. C offered D another glass. D declined, put down the book, left C alone. Now C sighed. Outside, the sound of the wood. C poured out more wine and picked up the paper and pen that had been bought as a present. C would write to S. D entered again: C had fallen. Would D like more wine? Yes. D put on the pullover. Cold. C thought how the pullover looked. They both read. C's was a novel, something with a pattern. Candles burned. One spluttered out. D drank wine until the bottle was finished and left C alone. C fell. D came in to draw the curtains and blow out the remaining candles. D loved the smell. The electric light was on, D turned that off too. D took the bottle. As C awoke, night turned and the hoo-hooing began again.

CHAPTER 131

The chairs comfortable. At 9 o'clock D came in and began to read the book on the table. C offered D wine. A glance around. C offered D another glass. D declined, put down the book, left C alone. Now C sighed. Outside, the sound of the wood. C poured out more wine and picked up the paper and pen that had been bought as a present. C would write to S. D entered again: C had fallen. Would D like more wine? Yes. D put on the pullover. Cold. C thought how the pullover looked. They both read. C's was a novel, something with a pattern. Candles burned. One spluttered out. D drank wine until the bottle was finished and left C alone, fell. D came in to draw the curtains and blow out the remaining candles. D loved the smell. The electric light was on, D turned that off too. D took the bottle. As C awoke, night turned and the hoo-hooing began

CHAPTER 132

The chairs comfortable. At 9 o'clock D came in and began to read the book on the table. C offered D wine. A glance around. C offered D another glass. D declined, put down the book, left C alone. Now C sighed. Outside, the sound of the wood. C poured out more wine and picked up the paper and pen that had been bought as a present. C would write to S. D entered again: C had fallen. Would D like more wine? Yes. D put on the pullover. C thought how the pullover looked. They both read. C's was a novel, something with a pattern. Candles burned. One spluttered out. D drank wine until the bottle was finished and left C alone, fell. D came in to draw the curtains and blow out the remaining candles. D loved the smell. The electric light was on, D turned that off too. D took the bottle. As C awoke, night turned and the hoo-hooing began again.

CHAPTER 133

At 9 o'clock D came in and began to read the book on the table. C offered D wine. A glance around. C offered D another glass. D declined, put down the book, left C alone. Now C sighed. Outside, the sound of the wood. C poured out more wine and picked up the paper and pen that had been bought as a present. C would write to S. D entered again: C had fallen. Would D like more wine? Yes. D put on the pullover. C thought how the pullover looked. They both read. C's was a novel, something with a pattern. Candles burned. One spluttered out. D drank wine until the bottle was finished and left C alone, fell. D came in to draw the curtains and blow out the remaining candles. D loved the smell. The electric light was on, D turned that off too. D took the bottle. As C awoke, night turned and the hoo-hooing began again.

CHAPTER 134

At 9 o'clock D came in and began to read the book on the table. C offered D wine. A glance around. C offered D another glass. D declined, put down the book, left C alone. Now C sighed. Outside, the sound of the wood. C poured out more wine and picked up the paper and pen that had been bought as a present. C would write to S. D entered again: C had fallen. Would D like more wine? Yes. D put on the pullover. C thought how the pullover looked. They both read. C's was a novel, something with a pattern. Candles burned. One spluttered out. D drank wine until the bottle was finished and left C alone. D came in to draw the curtains and blow out the remaining candles. D loved the smell. The electric light was on, D turned that off too. D took the bottle. As C awoke, night turned and the hoo-hooing began again.

CHAPTER 135

At 9 o'clock D came in and began to read the book on the table. C offered D wine. A glance around. C offered D another glass. D declined, put down the book, left C alone. Now C sighed. Outside, the sound of the wood. C poured out more wine and picked up the paper and pen that had been bought as a present. C would write to S. D entered again: C had fallen. Would D like more wine? Yes. D put on the pullover. C thought how the pullover looked. They both read. C's was a novel, something with a pattern. Candles burned, spluttered out. D drank wine until the bottle was finished and left C alone. D came in to draw the curtains and blow out the remaining candles. D loved the smell. The electric light was on, D turned that off too. D took the bottle. As C awoke, night turned and the hoo-hooing began again.

CHAPTER 136

At 9 o'clock D came in and began to read the book on the table. C offered D wine. A glance around. C offered D another glass. D declined, put down the book, left C alone. Now C sighed. Outside, the sound of the wood. C poured out more wine and picked up the paper and pen that had been bought as a present. C would write to S. D entered again: C had fallen. Would D like more wine? Yes. D put on the pullover. C thought how the pullover looked. They both read. C's was a novel, something with a pattern. Candles burned, spluttered out. D drank wine until the bottle was finished and left C alone. D came in to draw the curtains and blow out the remaining candles. D loved the smell. The electric light was on, D turned that off too, took the bottle. As C awoke, night turned and the hoo-hooing began again.

CHAPTER 137

At 9 o'clock D came in and began to read the book on the table. C offered D wine. A glance around. C offered D another glass. D declined, put down the book, left C alone. Now C sighed. Outside, the wood. C poured out more wine and picked up the paper and pen that had been bought as a present. C would write to S. D entered again: C had fallen. Would D like more wine? Yes. D put on the pullover. C thought how the pullover looked. They both read. C's was a novel, something with a pattern. Candles burned, spluttered out. D drank wine until the bottle was finished and left C alone. D came in to draw the curtains and blow out the remaining candles. D loved the smell. The electric light was on, D turned that off too, took the bottle. As C awoke, night turned

CHAPTER 138

At 9 o'clock D came in and began to read the book on the table. C offered D wine. A glance around. C offered D another glass. D declined, put down the book, left C alone. Now C sighed. Outside, the wood. C poured out more wine and picked up the paper and pen that had been bought as a present. C would write to S. D entered again: C had fallen. Would D like more wine? Yes. D put on the pullover. How the pullover looked! They both read. C's was a novel, something with a pattern. Candles burned, spluttered out. D drank wine until the bottle was finished and left C alone. D came in to draw the curtains and blow out the remaining candles. D loved the smell. The electric light was on, D turned that off too, took the bottle. As C awoke, night turned and the hoo-hooing began again.

CHAPTER 139

At 9 o'clock D came in and began to read the book on the table. C offered wine. A glance around. C offered D another glass. D declined, put down the book, left C alone. Now C sighed. Outside, the wood. C poured out more wine and picked up the paper and pen that had been bought as a present. C would write to S. D entered again: C had fallen. Would D like more wine? Yes. D put on the pullover. How the pullover looked! They both read. C's was a novel, something with a pattern. Candles burned, spluttered out. D drank wine until the bottle was finished and left C alone. D came in to draw the curtains and blow out the remaining candles. D loved the smell. The electric light was on, D turned that off too, took the bottle. As C awoke, night turned and the hoo-hooing began again.

CHAPTER 140

At 9 o'clock D came in and began to read the book on the table. C offered wine. A glance around. C offered D another glass. D declined, put down the book, left C alone. Now C sighed. Outside, the wood. C poured out more wine and picked up the paper and pen that had been bought as a present. C would write to S. D entered again: C had fallen. Would D like more wine? Yes. D put on the pullover. How the pullover looked! They both read. C's was a novel, something with a pattern. Candles burned, spluttered out. D drank wine until the bottle was finished and left C alone. D came in to draw the curtains and blow out the remaining candles. D, the smell. The electric light was on, D turned that off too, took the bottle. As C awoke, night turned and the hoo-hooing began again.

CHAPTER 141

At 9 o'clock D came in and began to read the book on the table. C offered wine. A glance around. C offered D another glass. D declined, put down the book, left C alone. Now C sighed. Outside, the wood. C poured out more wine and picked up the paper and pen that had been bought as a present. C would write to S. D entered again: C had fallen. Would D like more wine? Yes. D put on the pullover. How the pullover looked! They both read. C's was a novel, something with a pattern. Candles burned, spluttered out. D drank wine until the bottle was finished and left C alone. D came in to draw the curtains and blow out the remaining candles. D, the smell. The electric light was on, D turned that off too, took the bottle. As C awoke, night turned, the hoo-hooing began again.

CHAPTER 142

At 9 o'clock D came in and began to read the book on the table. C offered wine. A glance around. C offered D another glass. D declined, put down the book, left C alone. Now C sighed. Outside, the wood. C poured out more wine and picked up the paper and pen that had been bought as a present. C would write to S. D entered. C had fallen. Would D like more wine? Yes. D put on the pullover. How the pullover looked! They both read. C's was a novel, something with a pattern. Candles burned, spluttered out. D drank wine until the bottle was finished and left C alone. D came in to draw the curtains and blow out the remaining candles. D, the smell. The electric light was on, D turned that off too, took the bottle. As C awoke, night turned, the hoo-hooing began again.

CHAPTER 143

At 9 o'clock D came in and began to read the book on the table. C offered wine. A glance around. C offered D another glass. D declined, put down the book, left C alone. Now C sighed. Outside, the wood. C poured out more wine and picked up the paper and pen that had been bought as a present. C would write to S. D entered. C had fallen. Would D like more wine? Yes. D put on the pullover. How the pullover looked! They both read. C's was a novel, something with a pattern. Candles burned, spluttered out. D drank wine until the bottle was finished and left C alone. D came in to draw the curtains and blow out the remaining candles. D, the smell. The electric light was on, D turned that off too, took the bottle. As C awoke, night turned, the hoo-hooing

CHAPTER 144

At 9 o'clock D came in and began to read the book on the table. C offered wine. A glance around. C offered D another glass. D declined, put down the book, left C alone. Now C sighed. Outside, the wood. C poured out more wine and picked up the paper and pen that had been bought as a present. C would write to S. D entered. C had fallen. Would D like more wine? Yes. D put on the pullover. How the pullover looked! They both read. C's was a novel, something with a pattern. Candles burned, spluttered out. D drank wine until the bottle was finished and left C alone. D came in to draw the curtains and blow out the remaining candles. The smell. The electric light was on, D turned that off too, took the bottle. As C awoke, night turned, the hoo-hooing again.

CHAPTER 145

At 9 o'clock D came in and began to read the book on the table. C offered wine. A glance around. C offered D another glass. D declined, put down the book, left C alone. Now C sighed. Outside, the wood. C poured out more wine and picked up the paper and pen that had been bought as a present. C would write to S. D entered. C had fallen. Would D like more wine? Yes. D put on the pullover. How the pullover looked! They both read. C's was a novel, something with a pattern. Candles burned, spluttered out. D drank wine until the bottle was finished and left C alone. D came in to draw the curtains and blow out the remaining candles. The electric light was on, D turned that off too, took the bottle. As C awoke, night turned, the hoo-hooing again.

CHAPTER 146

At 9 o'clock D came in and began to read the book on the table. C offered wine. A glance around. C offered D another glass. D declined, put down the book, left C alone. Now C sighed. Outside, the wood. C poured out more wine and picked up the paper and pen that had been bought as a present. C would write to S. D entered. Would D like more wine? Yes. D put on the pullover. How the pullover looked! They both read. C's was a novel, something with a pattern. Candles burned, spluttered out. D drank wine until the bottle was finished and left C alone. D came in to draw the curtains and blow out the remaining candles. The electric light was on, D turned that off too, took the bottle. As C awoke, night turned - the hoo-hooing again.

CHAPTER 147

At 9 o'clock D came in and began to read on the table. C offered wine. A glance around. C offered D another glass. D declined, put down the book, left C alone. Now C sighed. Outside, the wood. C poured out more wine and picked up the paper and pen that had been bought as a present. C would write to S. D entered. Would D like more wine? Yes. D put on the pullover. How the pullover looked! They both read. C's was a novel, something with a pattern. Candles burned, spluttered out. D drank wine until the bottle was finished and left C alone. D came in to draw the curtains and blow out the remaining candles. The electric light was on, D turned that off too, took the bottle. As C awoke, night turned - the hoo-hooing again.

CHAPTER 148

At 9 o'clock D came in and began to read on the table. C offered wine. A glance around. C offered D another glass. D declined, put down the book, left C alone. Now C sighed. Outside, the wood. C poured out more wine and picked up the paper and pen that had been bought as a present. C would write to SD. Would D like more wine? Yes. D put on the pullover. How the pullover looked! They both read. C's was a novel, something with a pattern. Candles burned, spluttered out. D drank wine until the bottle was finished and left C alone. D came in to draw the curtains and blow out the remaining candles. The electric light was on, D turned that off too, took the bottle. As C awoke, night turned - the hoo-hooing again.

CHAPTER 149

At 9 o'clock D came in and began to read on the table. C offered wine. A glance around. C offered D another glass. D declined, put down the book, left C alone. Now C sighed. Outside, the wood. C poured out more wine and picked up the paper and pen that had been bought as a present. C would write to SD. Would D like more wine? Yes. D put on the pullover. How the pullover looked! They both read. C's was a novel, something with a pattern. Candles burned, spluttered out. D drank wine until the bottle was finished, left C alone. D came in to draw the curtains and blow out the remaining candles. The electric light was on, D turned that off too, took the bottle. As C awoke, night turned - the hoo-hooing again.

CHAPTER 150

9 o'clock, D came in and began to read on the table. C offered wine. A glance around. C offered D another glass. D declined, put down the book, left C alone. Now C sighed. Outside, the wood. C poured out more wine and picked up the paper and pen that had been bought as a present. C would write to SD. Would D like more wine? Yes. D put on the pullover. How the pullover looked! They both read. C's was a novel, something with a pattern. Candles burned, spluttered out. D drank wine until the bottle was finished, left C alone. D came in to draw the curtains and blow out the remaining candles. The electric light was on, D turned that off too, took the bottle. As C awoke, night turned - the hoo-hooing again.

CHAPTER 151

9 o'clock: D came in and read on the table. C offered wine. A glance around. C offered D another glass. D declined, put down the book, left C alone. Now C sighed. Outside, the wood. C poured out more wine and picked up the paper and pen that had been bought as a present. C would write to SD. Would D like more wine? Yes. D put on the pullover. How the pullover looked! They both read. C's was a novel, something with a pattern. Candles burned, spluttered out. D drank wine until the bottle was finished, left C alone. D came in to draw the curtains and blow out the remaining candles. The electric light was on, D turned that off too, took the bottle. As C awoke, night turned - the hoo-hooing again.

CHAPTER 152

9 o'clock: D came in and read on the table. C offered wine. A glance around. C offered D another glass. D declined, put down the book, left C alone. Now C sighed. Outside, the wood. C poured out more wine and picked up the paper and pen that had been bought as a present. C would write to SD. Would D like more wine? Yes. D put on the pullover. How the pullover looked! They both read. C's was a novel, something with a pattern. Candles burned, spluttered out. D drank wine until the bottle was finished, left C alone. D came in to draw the curtains and blow out the remaining candles. The electric light was on: D turned that off too, took the bottle. As C awoke, night turned: hoo-hooing again.

CHAPTER 153

9 o'clock: D came in and read on the table. C offered wine. A glance around. C offered D another glass. D declined, put down the book, left C alone. Now C sighed. Outside, the wood. C poured out more wine and picked up the paper and pen that had been bought. C would write to SD. Would D like more wine? Yes. D put on the pullover. How the pullover looked! They both read. C's was a novel, something with a pattern. Candles burned, spluttered out. D drank wine until the bottle was finished, left C alone. D came in to draw the curtains and blow out the remaining candles. The electric light was on: D turned that off too, took the bottle. As C awoke, night turned: hoo-hooing again.

CHAPTER 154

9 o'clock: D came in and read on the table. C offered wine. A glance around. C offered D another glass. D declined, put down the book, left C alone. Now C sighed. Outside, the wood. C poured out more wine and picked up the paper and pen that had been bought. C would write to SD. Would D like more wine? Yes. D put on the pullover. How the pullover looked! They both read. C's was a novel, something with a pattern. Candles burned, spluttered out. D drank wine until the bottle was finished, left C alone. D came in to draw the curtains and blow out the remaining candles. The electric light was on: D turned that off too. As C awoke, night turned: hoo-hooing again.

CHAPTER 155

9 o'clock: D came in and read on the table. C offered wine. A glance around. C offered another glass. D declined, put down the book, left C alone. Now C sighed. Outside, the wood. C poured out more wine and picked up the paper and pen that had been bought. C would write to SD. Would D like more wine? Yes. D put on the pullover. How the pullover looked! They both read. C's was a novel, something with a pattern. Candles burned, spluttered out. D drank wine until the bottle was finished, left C alone. D came in to draw the curtains and blow out the remaining candles. The electric light was on: D turned that off too. As C awoke, night turned: hoo-hooing again.

CHAPTER 156

9: D came in and read on the table. C offered wine. A glance around. C offered another glass. D declined, put down the book, left C alone. Now C sighed. Outside, the wood. C poured out more wine and picked up the paper and pen that had been bought. C would write to SD. Would D like more wine? Yes. D put on the pullover. How the pullover looked! They both read. C's was a novel, something with a pattern. Candles burned, spluttered out. D drank wine until the bottle was finished, left C alone. D came in to draw the curtains and blow out the remaining candles. The electric light was on: D turned that off too. As C awoke, night turned: hoo-hooing again.

CHAPTER 157

9: D came in and read. C offered wine. A glance around. C offered another glass. D declined, put down the book, left C alone. Now C sighed. Outside, the wood. C poured out more wine and picked up the paper and pen that had been bought. C would write to SD. Would D like more wine? Yes. D put on the pullover. How the pullover looked! They both read. C's was a novel, something with a pattern. Candles burned, spluttered out. D drank wine until the bottle was finished, left C alone. D came in to draw the curtains and blow out the remaining candles. The electric light was on: D turned that off too. As C awoke, night turned: hoo-hooing again.

CHAPTER 158

9: D came in and read. C offered wine. A glance around. C offered another glass. D declined, put down the book, left C alone. Now C sighed. Outside, the wood. C poured out more wine and picked up the paper and pen that had been bought. C would write to S. Would D like more wine? Yes. D put on the pullover. How the pullover looked! They both read. C's was a novel, something with a pattern. Candles burned, spluttered out. D drank wine until the bottle was finished, left C alone. D came in to draw the curtains and blow out the remaining candles. The electric light was on: D turned that off too. As C awoke, night turned: hoo-hooing again.

CHAPTER 159

9: D came in and read. C offered wine. A glance around. C offered another glass. D declined, put down the book, left C alone. Now C sighed. Outside, the wood. C poured out more wine and picked up the paper and pen that had been bought. C would write to S. Would D like more wine? Yes. D put on the pullover. How the pullover looked! They both read. C's was a novel, something with a pattern. Candles burned, spluttered out. D drank wine until the bottle was finished, left C alone. D came in to draw the curtains and blow out the remaining candles. The electric light was on: D turned that off too. As C awoke: night, hoo-hooing again.

9: D came in and read. C offered wine. A glance around. C offered another glass. D declined, put down the book, left C alone. Now C sighed. Outside, the wood. C poured out more wine; picked up the paper and pen that had been bought. C would write to S. Would D like more wine? Yes. D put on the pullover. How the pullover looked! They both read. C's was a novel, something with a pattern. Candles burned, spluttered out. D drank wine until the bottle was finished, left C alone. D came in to draw the curtains and blow out the remaining candles. The electric light was on: D turned that off too. As C awoke: night, hoo-hooing again.

CHAPTER 161

D came in and read. C offered wine. A glance around. C offered another glass. D declined, put down the book, left C alone. Now C sighed. Outside, the wood. C poured out more wine; picked up the paper and pen that had been bought. C would write to S. Would D like more wine? Yes. D put on the pullover. How the pullover looked! They both read. C's was a novel, something with a pattern. Candles burned, spluttered out. D drank wine until the bottle was finished, left C alone. D came in to draw the curtains and blow out the remaining candles. The electric light was on: D turned that off too. As C awoke: night, hoo-hooing again.

CHAPTER 162

D came in and read. C offered wine. A glance around. C offered another. D declined, put down the book, left C alone. Now C sighed. Outside, the wood. C poured out more wine; picked up the paper and pen that had been bought. C would write to S. Would D like more wine? Yes. D put on the pullover. How the pullover looked! They both read. C's was a novel, something with a pattern. Candles burned, spluttered out. D drank wine until the bottle was finished, left C alone. D came in to draw the curtains and blow out the remaining candles. The electric light was on: D turned that off too. As C awoke: night, hoo-hooing again.

CHAPTER 163

D came in and read. C offered wine. A glance around. C offered another. D declined, put down the book, left C alone. Now C sighed. Outside, the wood. C poured out more wine; picked up the paper and pen that had been bought. C would write to S. Would D like more wine? Yes. D put on the pullover. How they both read! C's was a novel, something with a pattern. Candles burned, spluttered out. D drank wine until the bottle was finished, left C alone. D came in to draw the curtains and blow out the remaining candles. The electric light was on: D turned that off too. As C awoke: night, hoo-hooing again.

CHAPTER 164

D came in and read. C offered wine. A glance around. C offered another. D declined, put down the book, left C alone. Now C sighed. Outside, the wood. C poured out more wine; picked up the paper and pen. C would write to S. Would D like more wine? Yes. D put on the pullover. How they both read! C's was a novel, something with a pattern. Candles burned, spluttered out. D drank wine until the bottle was finished, left C alone. D came in to draw the curtains and blow out the remaining candles. The electric light was on: D turned that off too. As C awoke: night, hoo-hooing again.

CHAPTER 165

D came in and read. C offered wine. A glance around. C offered another. D declined, put down the book, left C alone. Now C sighed. Outside, the wood. C poured out more wine; picked up the paper and pen. C would write to S. Would D like more wine? Yes. D put on the pullover. How they both read! C's was a novel, something with a pattern. Candles spluttered out. D drank wine until the bottle was finished, left C alone. D came in to draw the curtains and blow out the remaining candles. The electric light was on: D turned that off too. As C awoke: night, hoo-hooing again.

CHAPTER 166

D came in and read. C offered wine. A glance around. C offered another. D declined, put down the book, left C alone. Now C sighed. Outside, the wood. C poured out more wine; picked up the paper and pen. C would write to S. Would D like more wine? Yes. D put on the pullover. How they both read! C's was a novel, something with a pattern. Candles spluttered out. D drank wine until the bottle was finished, left C alone, came in to draw the curtains and blow out the remaining candles. The electric light was on: D turned that off too. As C awoke: night, hoo-hooing again.

CHAPTER 167

D came in and read. C offered wine. A glance around. C offered another. D declined, put down the book, left C alone. Now C sighed. Outside, the wood. C poured out more wine; picked up the paper and pen. C would write to S. Would D like more wine? Yes. D put on the pullover. How they both read! C's was a novel, something with a pattern. Candles spluttered out. D drank until the bottle was finished, left C alone, came in to draw the curtains and blow out the remaining candles. The electric light was on: D turned that off too. As C awoke: night, hoo-hooing again.

CHAPTER 168

D came in. C offered wine. A glance around. C offered another. D declined, put down the book, left C alone. Now C sighed. Outside, the wood. C poured out more wine; picked up the paper and pen. C would write to S. Would D like more wine? Yes. D put on the pullover. How they both read! C's was a novel, something with a pattern. Candles spluttered out. D drank until the bottle was finished, left C alone, came in to draw the curtains and blow out the remaining candles. The electric light was on: D turned that off too. As C awoke: night, hoo-hooing again.

CHAPTER 169

D came in. C offered wine. A glance around. C offered another. D declined, put down the book, left C. Now C sighed. Outside, the wood. C poured out more wine; picked up the paper and pen. C would write to S. Would D like more wine? Yes. D put on the pullover. How they both read! C's was a novel, something with a pattern. Candles spluttered out. D drank until the bottle was finished, left C alone, came in to draw the curtains and blow out the remaining candles. The electric light was on: D turned that off too. As C awoke: night, hoo-hooing again.

CHAPTER 170

D came in. C offered wine. A glance around. C offered another. D declined, put down the book, left C. Now C sighed. Outside, the wood. C poured out more wine; picked up the pen. C would write to S. Would D like more wine? Yes. D put on the pullover. How they both read! C's was a novel, something with a pattern. Candles spluttered out. D drank until the bottle was finished, left C alone, came in to draw the curtains and blow out the remaining candles. The electric light was on: D turned that off too. As C awoke: night, hoo-hooing again.

CHAPTER 171

D came in. C offered wine. A glance around. C offered another. D declined, put down the book, left C. Now C sighed. Outside, the wood. C poured out more wine; picked up the pen. C would write to S. Would D like more wine? Yes. D put on the pullover. How they both read! C's was a novel, something with a pattern. Candles spluttered. D drank until the bottle was finished, left C alone, came in to draw the curtains and blow out the remaining candles. The electric light was on: D turned that off too. As C awoke: night, hoo-hooing again.

CHAPTER 172

D came in. C offered wine. A glance around. C offered another. D declined, put down the book, left C. Now C sighed. Outside, the wood. C poured out more wine; picked up the pen. C would write to S. Would D like more wine? Yes. D put on the pullover. They both read! C's was a novel, something with a pattern. Candles spluttered. D drank until the bottle was finished, left C alone, came in to draw the curtains and blow out the remaining candles. The electric light was on: D turned that off too. As C awoke: night, hoo-hooing again.

CHAPTER 173

D came in. C offered wine. A glance around. C offered another. D declined, put down the book, left C. Now C sighed. Outside, the wood. C poured out more wine; picked up the pen. C would write to S. Would D like more? Yes. D put on the pullover. They both read! C's was a novel, something with a pattern. Candles spluttered. D drank until the bottle was finished, left C alone, came in to draw the curtains and blow out the remaining candles. The electric light was on: D turned that off too. As C awoke: night, hoo-hooing again.

CHAPTER 174

C offered wine. A glance around. C offered another. D declined, put down the book, left C. Now C sighed. Outside, the wood. C poured out more wine; picked up the pen. C would write to S. Would D like more? Yes. D put on the pullover. They both read. C's was a novel, something with a pattern. Candles spluttered. D drank until the bottle was finished, left C alone, came in to draw the curtains and blow out the remaining candles. The electric light was on: D turned that off too. As C awoke: night, hoo-hooing again.

CHAPTER 175

C offered wine. A glance around. C offered another. D declined, put down the book, left C. Now C sighed. Outside, the wood. C poured out more wine; picked up the pen. C would write to S. Would D like more? Yes. D put on the pullover. They both read. C's, a novel, something with a pattern. Candles spluttered. D drank until the bottle was finished, left C alone, came in to draw the curtains and blow out the remaining candles. The electric light was on: D turned that off too. As C awoke: night, hoo-hooing again.

CHAPTER 176

C offered wine. A glance around. C offered another. D declined, put down the book, left C. Now C sighed. Outside, the wood. C poured out more wine; picked up the pen. C would write to S. Would D like more? Yes. D put on the pullover. They read. C's, a novel, something with a pattern. Candles spluttered. D drank until the bottle was finished, left C alone, came in to draw the curtains and blow out the remaining candles. The electric light was on: D turned that off too. As C awoke: night, hoo-hooing again.

CHAPTER 177

C offered wine. A glance around. C offered another. D declined, put down the book, left. Now C sighed. Outside, the wood. C poured out more wine; picked up the pen. C would write to S. Would D like more? Yes. D put on the pullover. They read. C's, a novel, something with a pattern. Candles spluttered. D drank until the bottle was finished, left C alone, came in to draw the curtains and blow out the remaining candles. The electric light was on: D turned that off too. As C awoke: night, hoo-hooing again.

CHAPTER 178

C offered wine. A glance around. C offered another. D declined, put down the book, left. Now C sighed. Outside, C poured out more wine; picked up the pen. C would write to S. Would D like more? Yes. D put on the pullover. They read. C's, a novel, something with a pattern. Candles spluttered. D drank until the bottle was finished, left C alone, came in to draw the curtains and blow out the remaining candles. The electric light was on: D turned that off too. As C awoke: night, hoo-hooing again.

CHAPTER 179

C offered wine. A glance around. C offered another.
D declined, put down the book, left. Now C sighed.
Outside, C poured out more wine; picked up the pen. C
would write to S. Would D like more? Yes. D put on the
pullover. They read. C's novel; something with a pattern.
Candles spluttered. D drank until the bottle was finished,
left C alone, came in to draw the curtains and blow out
the remaining candles. The electric light was on: D turned
that off too. As C awoke: night, hoo-hooing again.

CHAPTER 180

C offered wine. A glance around. C offered another. D declined, put down the book. Now C sighed. Outside, C poured out more wine; picked up the pen. C would write to S. Would D like more? Yes. D put on the pullover. They read. C's novel; something with a pattern. Candles spluttered. D drank until the bottle was finished, left C alone, came in to draw the curtains and blow out the remaining candles. The electric light was on: D turned that off too. As C awoke: night, hoo-hooing again.

CHAPTER 181

C offered wine, a glance around, offered another. D declined, put down the book. Now C sighed. Outside, C poured out more wine; picked up the pen. C would write to S. Would D like more? Yes. D put on the pullover. They read. C's novel; something with a pattern. Candles spluttered. D drank until the bottle was finished, left C alone, came in to draw the curtains, blow out the remaining candles. The electric light was on: D turned that off too. As C awoke: night, hoo-hooing again.

CHAPTER 182

C offered wine, a glance around, offered another. D declined, put down the book. Now C sighed. Outside, C poured out more wine; picked up the pen. C would write S. Would D like more? Yes. D put on the pullover. They read. C's novel; something with a pattern. Candles spluttered. D drank until the bottle was finished, left C alone, came in to draw the curtains, blow out the remaining candles. The electric light was on: D turned that off too. As C awoke: night, hoo-hooing again.

CHAPTER 183

C offered wine, a glance around, offered another. D put down the book. Now C sighed. Outside, C poured out more wine; picked up the pen. C would write S. Would D like more? Yes. D put on the pullover. They read. C's novel; something with a pattern. Candles spluttered. D drank until the bottle was finished, left C alone, came in to draw the curtains, blow out the remaining candles. The electric light was on: D turned that off too. As C awoke: night, hoo-hooing again.

CHAPTER 184

C offered wine, a glance around, offered another. D put down the book. Now C sighed. Outside, C poured more wine; picked up the pen. C would write S. Would D like more? Yes. D put on the pullover. They read. C's novel; something with a pattern. Candles spluttered. D drank until the bottle was finished, left C alone, came in to draw the curtains, blow out the remaining candles. The electric light was on: D turned that off too. As C awoke: night, hoo-hooing again.

CHAPTER 185

C offered wine, a glance around, another. D put down the book. Now C sighed. Outside, C poured more wine; picked up the pen. C would write S. Would D like more? Yes. D put on the pullover. They read. C's novel; something with a pattern. Candles spluttered. D drank until the bottle was finished, left C alone, came in to draw the curtains, blow out the remaining candles. The electric light was on: D turned that off too. As C awoke:night, hoo-hooing again.

CHAPTER 186

C offered wine, a glance around, another. D put down the book. Now C sighed. Outside, C poured more wine; picked up the pen. C would write S. Would D like more? Yes. D put on the pullover. They read. C's novel; something with a pattern. Candles spluttered. D drank until the bottle was finished, left C alone, came in to draw the curtains, blow out the candles. The electric light was on: D turned that off too. As C awoke: night, hoo-hooing again.

CHAPTER 187

C offered wine, a glance around, another. D put down the book. C sighed. Outside, C poured more wine; picked up the pen. C would write S. Would D like more? Yes. D put on the pullover. They read. C's novel; something with a pattern. Candles spluttered. D drank until the bottle was finished, left C alone, came in to draw the curtains, blow out the candles. The electric light was on: D turned that off too. As C awoke: night, hoo-hooing again.

CHAPTER 188

C offered wine, a glance around. D put down the book. C sighed. Outside, C poured more wine; picked up the pen. C would write S. Would D like more? Yes. D put on the pullover. They read. C's novel; something with a pattern. Candles spluttered. D drank until the bottle was finished, left C alone, came in to draw the curtains, blow out the candles. The electric light was on: D turned that off too. As C awoke: night, hoo-hooing again.

CHAPTER 189

C offered wine, a glance around. D put down the book. C sighed. Outside, C poured more wine; picked up the pen. C would write S. Would D like more? Yes. D put on the pullover. They read. C's; something with a pattern. Candles spluttered. D drank until the bottle was finished, left C alone, came in to draw the curtains, blow out the candles. The electric light was on: D turned that off too. As C awoke: night, hoo-hooing again.

CHAPTER 190

C offered wine, a glance around. D put down the book. C sighed, C poured more wine, picked up the pen. C would write S. Would D like more? Yes. D put on the pullover. They read. C's; something with a pattern. Candles spluttered. D drank until the bottle was finished, left C alone, came in to draw the curtains, blow out the candles. The electric light was on: D turned that off too. As C awoke: night, hoo-hooing again.

CHAPTER 191

C offered wine, a glance around. D put down the book. C sighed, C poured more wine, picked up the pen, would write S. Would D like more? Yes. D put on the pullover. They read. C's; something with a pattern. Candles spluttered. D drank until the bottle was finished, left C alone, came in to draw the curtains, blow out the candles. The electric light was on: D turned that off too. As C awoke: night, hoo-hooing again.

CHAPTER 192

C offered wine, a glance around. D put down the book. C sighed, C poured more wine, picked up the pen, would write S. Would D like more? Yes. D put on the pullover. They read. C's; something with a pattern. Candles spluttered. D drank until the bottle was finished, left C alone, came in to draw the curtains, blow out the candles. The electric light was on: turned that off too. As C awoke: night, hoo-hooing again.

CHAPTER 193

C offered wine, a glance around. D put down the book. C sighed, C poured more wine, picked up the pen, would write S. Would D like more? Yes. D put on the pullover. They read. C's; something with a pattern. Candles spluttered. D drank until the bottle was finished, left C alone, came in to draw the curtains, blow out the candles. The electric light was on: turned that off too. C awoke: night, hoo-hooing again.

CHAPTER 194

C offered wine, a glance around. D put down the book. C sighed, C poured more wine, picked up the pen, would write S. Would D like more? Yes. D put on the pullover. They read. C's; something with a pattern. Candles spluttered. D drank until the bottle was finished. C alone, came in to draw the curtains, blow out the candles. The electric light was on: turned that off too. C awoke: night, hoo-hooing again.

CHAPTER 195

C offered wine, a glance around. D put down the book. C sighed, poured more wine, picked up the pen, would write S. Would D like more? Yes. D put on the pullover. They read. C's; something with a pattern. Candles spluttered. D drank until the bottle was finished. C alone, came in to draw the curtains, blow out the candles. The electric light was on: turned that off too. C awoke: night, hoo-hooing again.

CHAPTER 196

C offered wine, a glance around. D put down the book, sighed, poured more wine, picked up the pen, would write S. Would D like more? Yes. D put on the pullover. They read. C's; something with a pattern. Candles spluttered. D drank until the bottle was finished. C alone, came in to draw the curtains, blow out the candles. The electric light was on: turned that off too. C awoke: night, hoo-hooing again.

CHAPTER 197

C offered wine, a glance around. D put down the book, sighed, poured more wine, picked up the pen, would write S. Would D like more? Yes. D put on the pullover. They read. C's – something with a pattern. Candles spluttered. D drank. The bottle was finished. C alone, came in to draw the curtains, blow out the candles. The electric light was on: turned that off too. C awoke: night, hoo-hooing again.

CHAPTER 198

C offered wine, a glance around. D put down the book, sighed, poured more wine, picked up the pen, would write S. Would D like more? Yes. D put on the pullover. They read. C's – something with a pattern. Candles spluttered. D drank – the bottle finished. C alone, came in to draw the curtains, blow out the candles. The electric light was on: turned that off too. C awoke: night, hoo-hooing again.

CHAPTER 199

C offered wine, a glance around. D put down the book, sighed, poured more wine, picked up the pen. Would S, would D like more? Yes. D put on the pullover. They read. C's – something with a pattern. Candles spluttered. D drank – the bottle finished. C alone, came in to draw the curtains, blow out the candles. The electric light was on: turned that off too. C awoke: night, hoo-hooing again.

CHAPTER 200

C offered wine, a glance around, put down the book, sighed, poured more wine, picked up the pen. Would S, would D like more? Yes. D put on the pullover. They read. C's – something with a pattern. Candles spluttered. D drank – the bottle finished. C alone, came in to draw the curtains, blow out the candles. The electric light was on: turned that off too. C awoke: night, hoo-hooing again.

CHAPTER 201

C offered wine, a glance around, put down the book, sighed, poured more wine, picked up the pen. Would S, would D like more? D put on the pullover. They read. C's – something with a pattern. Candles spluttered. D drank – the bottle finished. C alone, came in to draw the curtains, blow out the candles. The electric light was on: turned that off too. C awoke: night, hoo-hooing again.

CHAPTER 202

C offered wine, a glance around, put down the book, sighed, poured more wine, picked up the pen. Would, would D like more? D put on the pullover. They read. C's – something with a pattern. Candles spluttered. D drank – the bottle finished. C alone, came in to draw the curtains, blow out the candles. The electric light was on: turned that off too. C awoke: night, hoo-hooing again.

CHAPTER 203

C offered wine, a glance around, put down the book, poured more wine, picked up the pen. Would, would D like more? D put on the pullover. They read. C's – something with a pattern. Candles spluttered. D drank – the bottle finished. C alone, came in to draw the curtains, blow out the candles. The electric light was on: turned that off too. C awoke: night, hoo-hooing again.

CHAPTER 204

C offered wine, a glance around, put down the book, poured more wine, picked up the pen. Would, would D like more? D put on the pullover. They read. C's – something with a pattern. Candles spluttered. D drank – the bottle finished. C alone, came in to draw the curtains, blow out the candles. The electric light was on: turned that off too. C awoke: hoo-hooing again.

CHAPTER 205

C offered wine, a glance around, put down the book, poured more wine, picked up the pen. Would D like more? D put on the pullover. They read. C's – something with a pattern. Candles spluttered. D drank – the bottle finished. C alone, came in to draw the curtains, blow out the candles. The electric light was on: turned that off too. C awoke: hoo-hooing again.

CHAPTER 206

C offered wine, a glance around, put down the book, poured more wine, picked up the pen. Would D like more? D put on the pullover. They read. Something with a pattern. Candles spluttered. D drank – the bottle finished. C alone, came in to draw the curtains, blow out the candles. The electric light was on: turned that off too. C awoke: hoo-hooing again.

CHAPTER 207

C offered wine, a glance around, put down the book, poured more wine, picked up the pen. Would D like more? D put on the pullover. They read. Something with a pattern. Candles. D drank – the bottle finished. C alone, came in to draw the curtains, blow out the candles. The electric light was on: turned that off too. C awoke: hoo-hooing again.

CHAPTER 208

C offered wine, a glance around, put down the book, poured more wine, picked up the pen. Would D like more? D put on the pullover. They read. Something with a pattern. Candles. Drank. The bottle finished. C alone, came in to draw the curtains, blow out the candles. The electric light was on: turned that off too. C awoke: hoo-hooing again.

CHAPTER 209

C offered wine, a glance around, put down the book, poured more wine, picked up the pen. Would D like more? D put on the pullover, read. Something with a pattern. Candles. Drank. The bottle finished. C alone, came in to draw the curtains, blow out the candles. The electric light was on: turned that off too. C awoke: hoo-hooing again.

CHAPTER 210

C offered wine, a glance around, put down the book, poured more wine, picked up the pen. Would D like more? D put on the pullover, read. Something with a pattern. Candles. The bottle finished. C alone, came in to draw the curtains, blow out the candles. The electric light was on: turned that off too. C awoke: hoo-hooing again.

CHAPTER 211

C offered wine, a glance around, put down the book, poured more wine, picked up the pen. Would D like more? D put on the pullover, read. Something with a pattern. Candles. The bottle finished. C alone, came in to draw the curtains, blow out candles. The electric light was on: turned that off too. C awoke: hoo-hooing again.

CHAPTER 212

C offered wine, a glance around, put down the book, poured more wine, picked up the pen. Would D like more? D put on the pullover, read. Something with a pattern. Candles. The bottle finished. C came in to draw the curtains, blow out candles. The electric light was on: turned that off too. C awoke: hoo-hooing again.

CHAPTER 213

C offered wine, a glance around, put down the book, poured more wine, picked up the pen. Would D like more? D put on the pullover, read with a pattern. Candles. The bottle finished. C came in to draw the curtains, blow out candles. The electric light was on: turned that off too. C awoke: hoo-hooing again.

CHAPTER 214

C offered wine, a glance around, put down the book, poured more wine, picked up the pen. Would D like more? D put on the pullover, read with a pattern. Candles. Bottle finished. C came in to draw the curtains, blow out candles. The electric light was on: turned that off too. C awoke: hoo-hooing again.

CHAPTER 215

C offered wine, a glance around, put down the book, poured more wine, picked up the pen. Would D like more? D put on the pullover, read with a pattern. Candles. Bottle finished. C came in to draw the curtains, blow out candles. The light was on: turned that off too. C awoke: hoo-hooing again.

CHAPTER 216

C offered wine, a glance around, put down the book, poured wine, picked up the pen. Would D like more? D put on the pullover, read with a pattern. Candles. Bottle finished. C came in to draw the curtains, blow out candles. The light was on: turned that off too. C awoke: hoo-hooing again.

CHAPTER 217

C offered wine, a glance around, put down the book, poured wine, picked up the pen. Would D like more? D put on the pullover, read with a pattern. Bottle finished. C came in to draw the curtains, blow out candles. The light was on: turned that off too. C awoke: hoo-hooing again.

CHAPTER 218

C offered wine, a glance around, put down the book, poured wine, picked up the pen. Would D like more? D put on the pullover, read with a pattern. Finished, C came in to draw the curtains, blow out candles. The light was on: turned that off too. C awoke: hoo-hooing again.

CHAPTER 219

C offered wine, a glance around, put down the book, poured wine, picked up the pen. Would D like more? D put on the pullover, read with a pattern. C came in to draw the curtains, blow out candles. The light was on: turned that off too. C awoke: hoo-hooing again.

CHAPTER 220

C offered wine, a glance around, put down the book, poured wine, picked up the pen. Would D like more? D put on the pullover, read with a pattern, came in to draw the curtains, blow out candles. The light was on: turned that off too. C awoke: hoo-hooing again.

CHAPTER 221

C offered wine around, put down the book, poured wine, picked up the pen. Would D like more? D put on the pullover, read with a pattern, came in to draw the curtains, blow out candles. The light was on: turned that off too. C awoke: hoo-hooing again.

CHAPTER 222

C offered wine around, put down the book,wine, picked up the pen. Would D like more? D put on the pullover, read with a pattern, came in to draw the curtains, blow out candles. The light was on: turned that off too. C awoke: hoo-hooing again.

CHAPTER 223

C offered wine around, put down the book, wine, picked up the pen. Would D like more? D put on the pullover with a pattern, came in to draw the curtains, blow out candles. The light was on: turned that off too. C awoke: hoo-hooing again.

CHAPTER 224

C offered wine around, put down the book, picked up the pen. Would D like more? D put on the pullover with a pattern, came in to draw the curtains, blow out candles. The light was on: turned that off too. C awoke: hoo-hooing again.

CHAPTER 225

C offered wine around, put down the book, picked up the pen. Would D like more? D put on the pullover with a pattern, came in to draw the curtains, blow out candles. The light on: turned that off too. C awoke: hoo-hooing again.

CHAPTER 226

C offered wine around, put down the book, picked up the pen. Would D like more? D put on the pullover with a pattern, came in to draw the curtains, blow out candles. The light on: turned off too. C awoke: hoo-hooing again.

CHAPTER 227

C offered wine around, put down the book, picked up the pen. Would D like more? D put on the pullover with a pattern, came in to draw the curtains, blow out candles. The light: turned off too. C awoke: hoo-hooing again.

CHAPTER 228

C offered wine around, put down the book, picked up the pen. Would D like more? D put on the pullover with a pattern, in to draw the curtains, blow out candles. The light: turned off too. C awoke: hoo-hooing again.

CHAPTER 229

C offered wine around, put down the book, picked up
the pen. Would D like more? D put on the pullover with
a pattern: in to draw the curtains, blow out candles. The
light off too. C awoke: hoo-hooing again.

CHAPTER 230

C offered wine around, put down the book, picked up the pen. More? D put on the pullover with a pattern: in to draw the curtains, blow out candles. The light off too. C awoke: hoo-hooing again.

CHAPTER 231

C offered wine around, put down the book, picked up the pen. More? D put on the pullover with a pattern: in to draw the curtains, blow out candles. The light off, C awoke: hoo-hooing again.

CHAPTER 232

C offered wine around, put down the book, picked up the pen. D put on the pullover with a pattern: in to draw the curtains, blow out candles. The light off, C awoke: hoo-hooing again.

CHAPTER 233

C offered wine around, put down the book, picked up the pen. D put on the pullover with a pattern: in to draw the curtains, blow out candles. The light off, C awoke: hoo-hooing.

CHAPTER 234

C offered wine, put down the book, picked up the pen. D put on the pullover with a pattern: in to draw the curtains, blow out candles. The light off, C awoke: hoo-hooing.

CHAPTER 235

C offered wine, put down the book, picked up the pen. D put on the pullover with a pattern: in to draw the curtains, blow out candles. The light off, awoke: hoo-hooing.

CHAPTER 236

C offered wine, put down the book, picked up the pen, put on the pullover with a pattern: in to draw the curtains, blow out candles. The light off, awoke: hoo-hooing.

CHAPTER 237

C offered wine, put down the book, picked up the pen, put on the pullover with a pattern: in to draw curtains, blow out candles. The light off, awoke: hoo-hooing.

CHAPTER 238

C offered wine, put down the book, picked up the pen, put on the pullover with a pattern: in to draw curtains, blow out candles. The light – awoke – hoo-hooing.

CHAPTER 239

C offered wine, put down the book, picked up the pen,
put on the pullover with a pattern: in to draw curtains,
blow candles. The light – awoke – hoo-hooing.

CHAPTER 240

C offered wine, put down the book, the pen, put on the pullover with a pattern: in to draw curtains, blow candles. The light – awoke – hoo-hooing.

CHAPTER 241

C offered wine, put down the book, the pen, put on the
pullover with a pattern: in to draw curtains, blow candles.
The light, hoo-hooing.

CHAPTER 242

C offered wine, put down the book, pen, put on the pullover with a pattern: in to draw curtains, blow candles. The light hoo-hooing.

CHAPTER 243

C offered wine, put down the book, pen, put on the pullover (a pattern), in to draw curtains, blow candles. The light hoo-hooing.

CHAPTER 244

C offered, put down the book, pen, put on the pullover (a pattern), in to draw curtains, blow candles. The light hoo-hooing.

CHAPTER 245

C offered, put down the pen, put on the pullover (a pattern), in to draw curtains, blow candles. The light hoo-hooing.

CHAPTER 246

C offered the pen, put on the pullover (a pattern), in to draw curtains, blow candles. The light hoo-hooing.

CHAPTER 247

C offered the pen, put on the pullover (a pattern). In to
draw curtains, candles. The light hoo-hooing.

CHAPTER 248

C offered the pen, put on the pullover (a pattern). In to draw curtains, candles. Light hoo-hooing.

CHAPTER 249

C offered the pen, the pullover (a pattern). In to draw curtains, candles. Light hoo-hooing.

CHAPTER 250

C offered the pen, the pullover (a pattern). In to draw curtains, light. Hoo-hooing.

CHAPTER 251

C offered the pen, the pullover (a pattern). In to draw light. Hoo-hooing.

CHAPTER 252

C, the pen, the pullover (a pattern). In to draw light. Hoo-hooing.

CHAPTER 253

C, the pen, the pullover (a pattern). In to draw hoo-hooing.

CHAPTER 254

C, the pen, the pullover (a pattern). In. Hoo-hooing.

CHAPTER 255

The pen, the pullover (a pattern). In. Hoo-hooing.

CHAPTER 256

The pen, the pullover (a pattern). Hoo-hooing.

CHAPTER 257

The pen, the pullover (a pattern).

CHAPTER 258

The pen, pullover (a pattern).

CHAPTER 259

The pen (a pattern).

CHAPTER 260

The pattern.

CHAPTER 261

Pattern.

James Davies is the author of the novel *When Two Are In Love* or *As I Came To Behind Frank's Transporter* co-written with Philip Terry, the short story *Changing Piece* and several poetry collections including *Plants*, *A Dog* and *stack*. For a number of years he organised the important event series The Other Room with Tom Jenks and Scott Thurston and continues to run his long-running and influential poetry press *if p then q*. Between 2017-18 he was Poet in Residence at The University of Surrey.

Printed in Great Britain
by Amazon